DARE TO SUC

The Dare Series 2

Dixie Lynn Dwyer

MENAGE EVERLASTING

Siren Publishing, Inc.
www.SirenPublishing.com

A SIREN PUBLISHING BOOK
IMPRINT: Ménage Everlasting

DARE TO SUCCEED
Copyright © 2015 by Dixie Lynn Dwyer

ISBN: 978-1-63259-759-5

First Printing: August 2015

Cover design by Les Byerly
All art and logo copyright © 2015 by Siren Publishing, Inc.

Printed in the U.S.A.

PUBLISHER
Siren Publishing, Inc.
www.SirenPublishing.com

DEDICATION

Dear readers.

Thank you for purchasing this legal copy of Dare to Succeed.

Life can be difficult enough to live and succeed in. Throw in being harassed and controlled by an ex-lover and your own brother, and you've got the formula for heart ache and disaster.

When Alicia gets to the town called Chance and makes new friends, she also begins to rebuild her life and her self-confidence. But she needs reassurance, support and people she can trust. Caldwell, Max and Monroe are three brothers set out to gain her trust and ultimately her heart. The last thing she expected was to find success, find strength, and ultimately find love in the arms of three brothers despite her painful past. May you enjoy their journey and Alicia's ultimate fight for freedom and success.

Happy Reading,

Hugs!

~Dixie~

DARE TO SUCCEED

The Dare Series 2

DIXIE LYNN DWYER

Prologue

Alicia Waltz meticulously sealed the final piece to her newest stained glass mosaic. She smiled as she lifted the 12 x 14 piece up against the sunlight watching the glow of numerous colors shine through. It was another masterpiece, a custom order from a Ms. Wynona Flood in San Francisco, California. "Thank you, eBay."

Alicia set it back down and then rolled her chair over toward the computer and created the e-mail and invoice for the order. She printed out the eBay receipt and shipping label then rolled back over toward the table and gathered the shipping supplies. She had a method to securing the packages and ensuring that each handmade piece made it to the customer in perfect condition. She even applied thin, hard pieces of wood around the cushioning of the frame to ensure it wouldn't get cracked or broken in transport. Once she secured the package and labeled it, she stood up and prepared to head into town to the post office.

Her phone rang. She reached out to read the caller ID and she felt her chest tighten. *Tony. Damn it, what does he want? Why can't he just leave me alone?*

She felt that sensation in her gut, the one that pushed her to ignore his calls, ignore his ability to control her still, after all he did, but she couldn't. She picked up the phone.

"Hello."

"Darling, how are you? It took you a while to pick up. Is everything okay?" he asked and she rolled her eyes as she glanced at herself in the mirror.

"Everything is fine, Tony. I was just in the other room and couldn't get to the phone fast enough. What's going on?" she asked, although she didn't even care. He was successful and making good money off investments and schmoozing the right people. After all, he took the money from the store he sold out from underneath her and reinvested it into stocks and trades he was tipped off on. Did he give her any of it? Hell no. He kept pushing it off and saying he was letting the money sit and ride the market. Meanwhile he had a new sports car, a new townhouse, new women, and she was left struggling to make ends meet, to save what she could and to continue hustling for every penny.

Asshole.

Alicia looked at herself in the mirror before slipping on her tennis shoes and smoothing out her floral skirt. She pulled the white sheer blouse off the hanger and placed it over the tan camisole she wore. She hadn't wanted to take the chance of getting anything on it while she worked.

"Nothing is going on. I just wanted to check in on you. Your brother said he tried to call you a few times and you haven't responded."

She was shocked. Her brother held allegiance to Tony despite everything he did to her. That was why she wasn't bothering speaking to her brother so much. She loved her brother Alvin, but he took Tony's side over hers every time. She was sick of it. Tony had a way of manipulating everyone he met. She wanted to be done with him. Why couldn't she just blow him off?

"Your silence tells me that you know you should call Alvin. He loves you, darling. He cares about you just like I do."

"Tony, we're not an item any more. I think—"

"You don't know what's good for you, Alicia. You never did. It's like you can't grow up and take charge of your life and the choices you make. You need Alvin and me to help you."

He cut her off and rambled on about her needing him.

I don't need you or Alvin. You're a manipulating asshole who screwed me over in every possible way. You piece of crap weasel.

"Are you listening to me, Alicia? You need to call your brother. Now, as soon as we hang up. He's worried about you. He was going to drive out there to that little town you've disappeared to. God, you better still have that great body of yours. That town sounds like the place rednecks wearing plaid and dirty sweatpants roam around in. You're too pretty for that. Do you need a little money or something? You're not still doing the eBay thing are you?"

"Well, actually I am and I'm doing very well—"

"You need to get a real job. Some of the investments are paying off a little. There are charges to remove money early but if you're willing to pay the fees then I can give you some of the money."

Pay the fees? That's my money, too, and you want me to pay the fees and you take more of the money? God, I need to tell him off. I need to get him out of my head and get over the fact I lost my virginity to him. He doesn't love me. He never did and never will. No one can love me. I don't have what it takes.

"I don't need any money. I'm doing fine. Listen, I need to go."

"You'll listen to me, Alicia. You know that I know best. Call Alvin. I'll check up with you in a few days."

The line went dead. He didn't even give her the chance to respond, never mind the chance to hang up first.

She growled as she put the phone down.

"Why do I let him get away with this? Why?" she asked aloud then looked in the mirror.

She hadn't lost her great figure, probably because she was stressed all the time, and filled with excess energy working out, running, then sleeping very little, all because of her past. Why did Tony still have such a hold on her? Why when she looked into the mirror she saw a failure, someone who needed Tony and her brother to guide her and support her? She wished that Alvin would support her as her brother and the only family she had, but he was caught up in his own corporate world. He'd gone through two divorces and he thought he had all the answers for her. His idea of her being successful and happy was her being married to Tony and being at Tony's command. Little did her brother know that Tony was a liar, a thief, a manipulator, and a cheat. Her brother was fooled by Tony. For all she knew Alvin probably owed Tony money, too. Maybe that was why Alvin was always asking her about her finances and about getting money from Tony after he sold their business? Why couldn't they just leave her alone?

She had truly loved the small gift shop, and as soon as she started adding her own stained glass pieces to the inventory the orders began to start. Tony didn't even care. It was like one day the store was theirs and thriving with potential, and the next day it was gone. Sold and without her knowledge. She couldn't believe that she almost got engaged to the man. He didn't even care about her designs and her love of creating stained glass artwork. He destroyed the trust she gave him. She wouldn't trust so easily ever again.

She looked at the package and took a deep breath. Her excited feelings in completing such a beautiful piece lessened after the call from Tony. He'd never believed in her talent and ability. He'd never accepted her insight into the small business they owned. All he wanted was her money and when they established the little storefront on a tourist strip in Dallas, it could have been a gold mine, their gold mine, but he had other plans. He sold it out from underneath her. She had been stupid. Falling in love with him. Trusting him as the contracts for the business were made and things took off. It was all in his name and under his power to sell. Even though it was a large chunk of her money that was used to get the loan started, he convinced her that it was better to be in his name so if the business failed her credit wouldn't be ruined. He always acted like he was putting her first, and it was too late when she realized he put himself first. Everything Tony did was for Tony.

She couldn't do a damn thing about it, but the money made from selling it was significant and he reinvested it. He tricked her into believing his ideas were best and she signed where he told her, trusting him, believing he was her everything. Meanwhile, he was cheating on her with other women, and using money to live the life of a bachelor. Fighting with him and Alvin got her nowhere. She left Dallas in hopes to start over and take control of her life. She should change her phone number so Tony couldn't call her.

She couldn't. They would worry. They would head out here and the last thing she needed was a confrontation with them. They would flip out about her living arrangements over a garage. They would minimize her business and her art. They would put down her friends and the lifestyles here in Chance. They would insult her, beat her down, and ultimately make her leave Chance. So she would continue to appease their phone calls and their belief they still held control over her. Maybe one day she would have the self-confidence and ability to break free, but for now, she would roll with the punches and do what she loved. Create stained glass pieces with the hope to one day open her own storefront and be successful. A pipe dream? Probably, but she had to have something to hold onto, some hope, some goal, or life just wasn't worth living and waking up every day for.

She grabbed her keys, her purse, and the nicely packaged stained glass mosaic and headed out the door. As she walked down the long flight of stairs above Dr. Anders's garage, she noticed his wife Lisa Marie and her other husband, Troy, getting into the car.

"Good morning," she called out and both of them smiled. Mrs. Anders was beaming. She was expecting another baby in just a few months. It was their third.

"Good morning, Alicia. Is that another brilliant creation of yours that you're shipping out?" Lisa Marie asked.

Alicia smiled as she joined them. "Sure is."

"I hope you took a picture of that one, too. I love seeing the finished product," Lisa Marie said.

"I did. Are you off to the doctor's office?" Alicia asked.

Lisa Marie smiled.

"Sure am, although my husband assures me all is well. I think he likes me coming into town to his office and handling everything in a professional manner. He should know by now after two babies that I'm going to try and deliver natural and with a midwife. Clara is exceptional."

"She sure is. I heard that Monica had some trouble with her delivery and Clara was able to help immensely. I think Dr. Anders just likes to show off his beautiful wife and how fit and amazing you look. I don't know how you do it."

"Thanks. Good luck with the piece, and send me the picture of it through the cell, okay?"

"Sure thing. Have a great day," Alicia said to them and then made her way to her own small car parked on the side of the garage.

The apartment she rented from the Anders was beautiful. It sat above their two-car garage and overlooked the back meadows of their home. It was an ideal location with a separate room filled with windows for her to create an art studio for her work.

Alicia headed down the road and toward town. Once she got this delivered she planned on stopping by the diner to talk with Marlena She was working a couple of days a week now. Her men didn't want her working so many hours.

Once she got to town she found a parking spot and then walked around to her trunk to get the package out.

"Need some help with that, ma'am?"

She heard the voice and immediately recognized it as Caldwell's. How did she not see him before she opened her trunk? She looked up, and up, finally finding his eyes then having to place her hand over her eyes to shield the sun.

"Oh, hello, Caldwell. I'm good. But thank you," she said and then leaned forward to get the long well-packaged box out of her trunk. She went to close the trunk but Caldwell did it for her. She gave him a small smile and tried to ignore the pull she had toward the man. He, like his brothers, Monroe and Sheriff Max Gordon, seemed to have an effect on her like no other men ever in her life, but they were so hard, powerful, and tough. She shied away from them every time one of them came around her. She found the three men attractive, but so did most women in town and anyone passing through. She was sure they had their share of women. Hell, Monroe and Caldwell were away on business a lot and the sheriff, well, he oozed sex appeal. She often wished they didn't intimidate her so much so that she could pick Monroe's and Caldwell's brains about business and how they succeeded, but that normal conversation would never happen. She was an introvert, thanks to Tony and her brother.

She started to walk.

"Finish another project?" he asked.

She nodded and they crossed the street together. He opened the post office door for her and she saw there was a little bit of a line.

"Selling to a gallery or was it an eBay order?" he asked.

She looked at him wondering why he even cared. He was just being polite.

"eBay order."

"Your work is exceptional, Alicia. You should be selling pieces in galleries and specialty stores. Hell, you should open your own store."

"Yeah right," she said and exhaled under her breath. The package was getting heavy, plus it was an awkward shape. She should pick his brain right now. *Funny that you say such a thing. It's something I've been contemplating. Any advice, Caldwell? Yeah right.*

She bit her tongue and leaned the package on her hip. *It's so heavy.*

"Don't sell yourself short. You should consider it."

"I have considered it. I've even thought of opening up something small in town, but my eBay earnings change from month to month. I need consistency before I make an investment like that."

"Well, maybe someone could back your investment. You know, like a business partner?"

She shook her head.

"I don't think so. I like to handle things on my own."

Thanks but no thanks. Been there, done that, and still trying to recover from the actions of my ex. The asshole. Never mind my own brother. The lazy man was always looking for the easy way out, and he thought she was it. Hell, Alvin still thinks that I'm going to take care of him by supporting him financially so he won't have to do shit. God forbid Alvin work a legitimate job and earn his own keep. No, instead he puts the pressure on me and cries about not finding work or getting hired and how I'm his sister and I should help him.

She felt guilty. Why should she feel guilty? She didn't do anything wrong. *God, I'm so screwed up.* She felt the tears hit her eyes and she quickly coughed, trying to cover up any indication that she was being emotional. Caldwell squinted at her. Had he seen the emotion in her eyes? Great, he would think something was wrong with her. Well, she was better off. He was out of her league in more ways than one.

She wouldn't tell Caldwell about Tony. After all it had been her insecurities, her lack of self-confidence and innocence that got her screwed, in more ways than just sexually. She lost her damn virginity to Tony. At least she didn't entirely regret that. Boy did Tony hold that over her head to this day. When she saw him last he even asked her if she were seeing anyone. God, she needed to gain a backbone when it came to Tony. Hell, when it came to men.

"I wouldn't write it off so quickly. A lot of people love your work and think you have a unique talent. You just need some marketing help, and maybe some promotional help, too."

It was her turn at the counter. She smiled at him. *Ask him for some advice. I'm safe here in the post office. Go ahead and ask him.*

"I'll think about it."

* * * *

Caldwell Gordon couldn't take his eyes off of Alicia. She was stunning and petite. Her head barely made it to his upper chest. Her femininity, shyness, and near insecurity made him have an instant protectiveness over her. God only knew what she would say or do if she knew that him and his brothers were planning on staking a permanent claim over her. Having to watch over her for the week a couple of months back had solidified their attraction to her, but she seemed unaffected. Perhaps she was just so shy she needed some persuading, but how could they persuade her to explore an attraction, if they couldn't get time alone to spend with her? He needed to think hard and come up with something good.

She looked so sad today. Every time he saw her he got this feeling that she wanted to say something to him but then she didn't. He could see the flash of emotion across her eyes and then a blank expression. She even opened her mouth to say something and then coughed or pretended to. What was she afraid of? Did he intimidate her? *God, I hope not.*

As he watched her process her newest order he thought about her craft, her unique ability to create such gorgeous colors and designs with stained glass pieces. Their new wine cellar was nearly complete in their own basement at home, but there was a large window that sat in the middle of the room that could use something unique. The thought hit him quickly. He could ask Alicia to take a look at it and see if she could design and work on the window at their home. That could give them a chance to get to know her and to make her feel more comfortable with them. It was worth the try. Especially staring at her back right now, looking over her sexy figure, her long brown hair, and listening to her sweet, quiet voice as she spoke with Lenny behind the counter.

He needed to make a move.

"So it should get to California by Friday. Is that good enough?" Lenny asked.

"Oh that's great. The customer hadn't expected it until almost a week later but I had time to complete it. Thanks, Lenny. Have a great day."

"You, too, Alicia," Lenny said, and Caldwell could see the man's cheeks turning a shade of pink as he winked at their woman. She was their woman, whether she knew it yet or not.

Alicia turned around and headed toward the door and right past him.

"Alicia. Could you hold up a minute? I wanted to run something by you," Caldwell said. He acted all businesslike and he knew his tone grabbed her attention as she nodded and stood there looking intimidated. She was sweet. He could only imagine how submissive she would be in the bedroom as he asked her to touch him, kiss him, plant her pussy over his face as he devoured her sweet cream. God, the fantasies he had about her were beginning to feel real, but he knew they weren't. Hell, she could turn him and his brothers down flat. If that happened he would never be the same again. He adored her. She was everything he wanted in a woman, a wife. His brothers believed so, too. He needed to make her feel safe and comfortable. The attraction was there. It had to be.

He gave Lenny the small package and some letters that needed to go out. Lenny gave him an odd expression but Caldwell ignored him.

If the man liked Alicia and thought he had a chance with her, he would make sure he realized right now that Alicia was off limits.

Caldwell wrapped an arm over Alicia's shoulder as he walked her out.

"We'll talk outside. It's a gorgeous day out," he told her and felt her stiffen up as he touched her. They walked outside and she sidestepped out of his hold. He squinted at her and she shyly turned away. His cock hardened. *God, she's irresistible. Please let her be attracted to my brothers and me. We can't get her out of our heads.*

"What's going on, Caldwell?" she asked him and he crossed his arms in front of his chest and took in the sight of her. She smelled so good and looked so pretty in her skirt and blouse. How he would love to explore her skin.

"I was wondering if you could help me out with something."

She looked at him and nodded.

"My brothers and I just finished putting in a wine cellar, in the basement, and there is this big beautiful window in the center of the room and we were thinking of doing something to it to lessen the amount of sunlight entering the room but also enhance the feeling of being in a wine-tasting room. Do you think you could come by and take a look at it and perhaps create something in stained glass to enhance the room?"

Her cheeks turned a shade of red and she stared at him.

"I don't know. I usually don't do such large pieces."

"Well, there's a first time for everything and you are pretty talented. We'd pay you of course."

"So like a private job?"

"Yes."

"I don't know what I would charge you for it, Caldwell. It would depend on the size and exactly what you were looking for in the design."

"I know. That's why it would be great if you could stop over. Do you think sometime this week, maybe in the afternoon so that you could see how much sun comes through?"

"Can I think about it?"

"I won't take no for an answer. I know how talented you are. I won't hire anyone else to come in. I would really like you to come up with something."

She hesitated a few seconds and then said okay. He wanted to leap for joy. This was going to work out perfectly. They'd get her to their place, get her to accept the job, and then make sure each of them visited her and talked to her as she worked so she would be more comfortable with them. They could probably talk her into staying for dinner or sharing lunch? This was a great plan. His brothers would be thanking him. Big time.

"So how about tomorrow afternoon? Maybe around one?"

"Sounds good to me."

"Do you know where we live?"

"Of course I do."

He raised one of his eyebrows up at her. Did she already have feelings for them? Did she drive by their place to catch a glimpse of them? God he hoped so.

"It's the one with the very elaborate entryway built up with stone pillars. There's no other place like it around Chance," she said, bursting his pleasure bubble, but he recovered quickly. The sight of her hazel eyes alone did wonders to him.

"Great. So I'll see you tomorrow."

She said good-bye and then she walked toward the diner. He would call his brothers immediately and let them know his plan. They would be thanking him for this for a very long time.

* * * *

"Are you serious? He just asked you that?" Marlena asked her as Mercedes and Adele smiled wide.

"Yes. I was shocked. I guess there's a first time for everything. I've never done such a huge job before, and it sounds huge."

"You'll be working in their home. That means they'll be watching you, talking to you, and trying to make a move," Adele said.

"No. It's strictly business if I even take it. I want to feel them out."

"You want to do more to them than that. Why are you denying this opportunity?" Mercedes asked.

"It's not professional to like a client. It should remain businesslike."

"Yeah like that's going to happen. Caldwell, Monroe, and the sheriff have had their eyes on you since you moved here. What makes you think that you can keep this all business?" Marlena asked her.

"I need to. I would never mix personal life with business. I learned the hard way where that leads. Now that Caldwell asked me to do something at his home professionally I need to keep that line drawn. Besides, I don't want to get involved with another man. I want to build up my confidence and start establishing my own goals and achieve them."

"So let me get this straight. If they ask you out or want to pursue a relationship after you're working for them, you'll decline?" Mercedes asked her.

"Of course I will. I was taken advantage of once before. I won't let a man get in the way of my future and what I find happiness in. Monroe, Caldwell, and the sheriff are used to being in charge and running things. I'm not going to take any chances. It's business and that's it."

"Well good luck with that, Alicia. With those men, you're going to need it to resist their good looks, their superior personalities, and their sexy bodies," Adele told her.

"Thanks a lot. I appreciate the support," Alicia replied.

"Don't get all insulted. We're here to support you in everything you do. No sweat," Marlena said.

"Oh she'll be sweating. The moment one of the Gordon brothers shows up in the basement half-dressed and ready to taste more than the wine," Adele teased, and Marlena and Mercedes chuckled, but Alicia felt the sense of anxiety as crazy thoughts scattered in her head.

Could the Gordon men be up to something? Did they think she was weak, vulnerable, and easily manipulated? She felt her anger surge and then came a calmness that warned her that things could get intense. Especially since she was attracted to all three brothers already.

But they didn't share that same attraction. They just wanted to hire her to create the stained glass window, and nothing more. She could do that.

"Hey, don't freak out. I'm certain Caldwell's intentions are noble. Just take each day one at a time. Who knows, maybe this idea of yours to keep things strictly business will fail because you're so attracted to them," Marlena said to her.

Alicia shook her head. "Tony called me this morning."

"Damn, Alicia, why didn't you say something sooner? No wonder you're so down on yourself and the Gordon brother situation. What did that jerk say to you? Why did he call?" Mercedes asked.

"To tell me to call my brother. I haven't returned any of Alvin's calls."

"Why not?" Adele asked her.

Alicia ran her finger over the rim of the iced tea glass. "Because when I talk to him he tells me all about Tony's successes and how I screwed up. He then tells me how he's low on money and that if I got involved with Tony again that Tony could help him out financially."

"That's ridiculous. What does he want you to do, sleep with Tony so he can get some money? That's screwed up, Alicia. You know that, right?" Mercedes asked.

"Yes, I know it is, but then Alvin starts in on our parents being dead and how he took such good care of me and raised me hoping that I would marry Tony so that I would be taken care of."

"And him, too, apparently. Your brother still messing around with fast payoff jobs?" Adele asked.

"I don't know. I don't want to know. I just want to be left alone so I can try and do what I want and what makes me happy," Alicia told them.

"Then being alone, being afraid to like another man or men is silly. Perhaps if things work out and you meet someone else, maybe that will finally send a message to Tony and your brother that you're no longer their little puppet? That you've moved on and are making your own decisions with your own life," Mercedes added.

"Maybe, but when I think about letting my guard down, I panic and that's no way to win a man's love. Trust needs to be proven first. I don't think I have the strength to be bothered."

"I think you do. I just think it will take the right man or men to help you realize you're special and that they are willing to do whatever you need for them to prove they love you and aren't going to hurt you. But you also need to take that chance. How else are you going to succeed in business and in your personal life? Don't sell yourself short. You're amazing. As soon as you realize that, then maybe you can achieve your goals and the happiness you're looking for," Marlena told her and she nodded her head.

Marlena was right, but it was easy for her to say. She'd landed three amazing men that adored her. Alicia didn't think she could be so lucky. Not with all the baggage, and her ex still in her life along with her controlling brother.

Chapter 1

"So things are going smoothly and we should be ready to pour concrete in another week," Richie Ray told Monroe Gordon.

"That's right on schedule. Excellent. Hopefully within the next few weeks my brother and I will have every storefront sold," Monroe replied as he looked around the new construction site on the edge of town in Chance. It was going to be sensational and people would love the cobblestone lined walkways, the lighted lampposts and all the little gardens that lined the walkways between store fronts. There were even going to be places to sit and rest, grab a coffee, some ice cream or other specialty foods from the local storefronts. It was like an additional shopping strip to Chance with unique stores.

"There's no doubt in my mind about that, Monroe. You and Caldwell have the ability to sell anything. Plus this site is perfect just like you said months ago. Chance is going to be growing in leaps and bounds," Richie Ray replied.

"It will grow as fast as the sheriff and the town board allow it to."

"Well having your brother as the sheriff must help. Besides, what you and Caldwell are doing is really admirable. To give fifty percent of the sale price to the local veterans in need will be a great help. A lot of our friends and their families are suffering."

"You don't have to tell me. I see it all the time."

"And that's also why you hired Ferguson construction for the brunt of the work here. Will, Leo, and Hank went through hell only a few years back."

"Indeed. They're good men and they do excellent work. So keep me abreast of the progress. I'll have a few business people interested in investing in some of the storefronts coming by next week. Seeing the foundation is a lot more appealing than piles of dirt and debris being pushed around."

Richie chuckled. "No problem. Talk to you soon."

Monroe disconnected the call and took a sip from his coffee cup. Things were going according to schedule so that was perfect. He had a few different buyers confirming contracts and playing out their designs for their stores. A florist, a clothing boutique, a pizza place, an ice cream and sweets parlor, a salon, and even a small organic grocer and vitamin shop. They just needed something special, something unique that could draw more people to shop there and to be a highlight of Chance.

His phone rang, interrupting his thoughts.

"Hey, bro, what's up?" Monroe asked Caldwell.

"A lot. You'll never guess who I bumped into in town."

"Who?"

"Alicia."

Monroe felt his chest tighten as he sat forward in his chair to listen to his brother. Months ago, when she first arrived in Chance, they each caught sight of her at separate times and were interested. A couple of months back they had to provide precautionary protection for her because her friend Marlena had some trouble. In that week he and his brothers felt even more of an attraction, but Alicia wasn't responsive. She was shy, petite, quiet, and seemed a bit on edge. That just seemed to interest them more.

"So did you actually speak to her?"

"I did better than that. I had a great idea. You know how we have been debating about what to do with that large window downstairs, and you know how Alicia creates those one-of-a-kind stained glass mosaics and scenes? Well I thought—"

"That she could make something custom for us where she would work from our home and where we could make her feel more comfortable and perhaps see if she's attracted to us, too."

"Exactly. Interestingly enough, I asked her about opening up her own storefront and selling her creations. She seemed cautious in her response and when I mentioned someone backing her up financially like a partner she all of about smashed that idea. I wonder if your theory about her trying and failing at a business was accurate. Maybe someone hurt her. I don't know, but since she said yes to coming by our place and seeing the potential job, I'll take it and see where it leads for us."

"That does sound promising and intriguing. We can push for more info as she gets comfortable," Monroe said.

"If she takes the job. She didn't seem too enthusiastic about it."

"Well if what we think is true and that someone hurt her or that she has financial problems then we'll find out and we'll help her. She's the kind of young woman that needs reassurance and to feel she can trust the people she is with. Why do you think she's always with Marlena, Mercedes, and Adele? They're all pretty quiet and shy."

"Well, this is our opportunity to let her get to know us. So, what else is going on? How is the construction going? Have you spoken to Richie?"

"Sure did. Looks like the foundations will be poured next week. I need to talk with Hank about some aspects of the construction. The Gianero family that is opening up the pizza parlor and small restaurant would like to have a second floor and balcony overlooking the streets in the front and the gardens in the back. I think it's possible but we'd have to alter some of the other designs a bit. Maybe change up the final drawings. I kind of like the idea."

Caldwell chuckled.

"Well, Hank is the one to talk to. I guess I'll catch up with you later. I want to go over the landscape proposals and designs to see how we're going to do the layout. I'll send you over anything I need confirmation on."

"I'll be back at the house by late afternoon. I have some meetings and some calls to make."

"No problem. Catch ya later."

Monroe smiled as he leaned back in his chair. Caldwell got them the opportunity they'd been waiting for. Alicia was going to be coming to their home and possibly working there. What better opportunity to get to know her and for her to get to know them. She should feel comfortable and at ease in no time. He felt the excitement immediately. He'd never felt like this before. Monroe never liked a woman so instantly and never one that wasn't throwing herself at him and his brothers. Alicia was different. She was sweet, sincere, and seemed timid. He felt an instant protectiveness over her just like his brothers did. He had to make sure that things went right. She was perfect for them and they needed to prove that to her.

* * * *

Alicia stared at the construction site from the hilltop down the street. She jogged here, just like she did every Wednesday and Friday before work. It was so exciting to see them begin to lay out the site and plan where the buildings would sit. She imagined what the strip on the outskirts of Chance would look like once they were complete. The town was expanding, and who knew how many more residents and storefronts there would be. This location could be prime. She just knew it.

She swallowed the lump of emotions in her throat along with the sensations of anxiety. She knew in her heart that this could be a great opportunity, yet every time she considered taking that next step to achieve her lifelong goal of being a storeowner and entrepreneur, she thought about Tony and what he had done to her. Hell, she thought about the criticism she would receive from him and how he would have the gall to come out here and insult her or worse, see the potential in the area and in her store and try to push his way in. As much as she wanted to believe she'd have the nerve to tell him no, she knew otherwise. Once he got Alvin involved and they tag-teamed her, she would collapse under their control.

Her vision blurred from filling with tears as she thought about Tony, thoughts of him taking over her ideas and ultimately owning her. In a lot of ways Tony believed he did own her. When he said she was special, and that there would always be a special place in his heart for her, she knew it was his way of saying he owned her. A part of her at least that no other man could ever have. Her virginity. He was so screwed up for doing that. Why couldn't he just let her go? He was the one that cheated on her. She recalled seeing that jerk just a month ago while at a convention in Dallas. He was so pompous and acted like he had every right to touch her, to flirt and behave like she had been so important to him at one time. He even suggested going up to his hotel room and "talking." She almost fell for his lies, but the creepy way he made her feel when he touched her or caressed her arm made her push him away and head home early. He was such a controlling, slimy skunk. How could she have been so stupid?

Then she realized, as she watched him mix and mingle, that he was like that with all women. He flirted, he seduced, he manipulated, and she saw him in action. Why did he have such a hold on her? She knew she needed to ignore his advances, and his hurtful comments that always seemed to hit her so hard. How did he have the ability to make her feel weak and not good enough?

Because he took my virginity? Who the hell cares? Plenty of women have multiple sexual partners before they find that special one. Why should it be different for me? He destroyed my confidence and til this day I can't make a firm decision on my own. I just keep working, creating my stained glass pieces, and hope to get discovered. That might never happen.

She came back from that trip frustrated, but also hurt. She had thought that she loved Tony and he loved her. They talked about their dreams and investments together. They seemed to be on the same page and equally determined. He built her up. He made her believe in herself and when she felt as if she were flying, heading toward success, he pulled the rug out from underneath her in more ways than one. Aside from the material things—the business sold out from underneath her, the future and her career—he tore her heart out. Even after time had passed and she saw him, Tony had a way of making her feel like somehow she was to blame. Like without him she couldn't succeed. Deep down she knew it wasn't right, but her self-confidence withered. Seeing him a month ago she realized that Tony still had a hold of her. That he could make her question her own judgment, her own decisions and her own capabilities. It didn't help that Tony was her brother's best friend.

Her brother, Alvin, hadn't been much help when things went wrong. Alvin thought the world of Tony. When Tony said that the buyout was out of his control, her brother believed him. Alvin saw Alicia as weak, passive and unable to do anything on her own. That was what got her to finally leave Dallas and head this way. Finding Chance where no one knew her or where she came from gained her the ability to be more independent and prove she didn't need Tony or anyone else to succeed in life. That was the plan, but looking at the construction again, feeling the determination to give this risk a try on her own, had her shaking in her sneakers and wondering if she were cut out to be anything other than Alicia Waltz, eBay shop owner of stained glass art work.

She thought about Caldwell and how she was supposed to meet him and his brothers at their house today. She didn't think it was a good idea, but she could use the money. She had enough set aside to rent a new building on the site she stared at in front of her. If only she had the courage and drive. Where had that drive gone? That determination, that pride and self-confidence in her art and her own capabilities?

She knew the answer. She lost focus. She allowed the past to still hold power of her now and nothing seemed to help her get through those walls and fight. Nothing.

Feeling defeated and emotional, she took a deep breath and prepared to head back to reality. She was nervous. She didn't know what to expect going to the home of three men who individually represented qualities, personalities, and abilities she feared. Why had she said yes to going? Why?

She stood up, stretched out her legs, and prepared for the run back home to her studio and two-bedroom loft above Dr. Anders's garage. His wife, Lisa Marie, and his brothers, Mitchel and Troy, were friendly, likable people. They had the kind of relationship that ran rampant around Chance. Alicia was envious in many ways.

Alicia smiled to herself. It was amazing how many ménage relationships she had been exposed to coming to Chance. It seemed like those involved with them were so happy. Like they found their perfect matches and truly adored one another. That was something else she could never have. A relationship with a man or men where she felt she could trust them fully without constantly fearing and worrying about when they would hurt her or disappoint her, never mind leave her. Tony did some serious damage to her heart and her confidence. She knew that, but in a way it made her more aware, maybe even more analytical of men in general. She took them as she saw them, and if she got a funny sensation in her gut, she ran as far as she could.

She placed her earbuds back into her ears then pressed the button on her small clip on iPod. The pop music filled her ears and she prepared for the four-mile run back home. She thought about the construction site and picked up speed heading down toward the roadway. The trees lined the road and she would need to slow down to take the blacktop the rest of the way back toward Chance. She was running so fast, too absorbed in the loud music and not paying any attention to anything else. As she ran down the hill and toward the roadway, she never expected to see the sheriff's patrol truck, and he apparently didn't expect someone to come running from the trees and straight into the road in front of his truck.

The loud screeching sound pulled her from her daze and she jerked to the right at the same time then jumped and tumbled out of the way and down into the dirt.

She felt the sting to her thigh and the hard thump to the roadway as she cried out.

She knew she was cut and scraped up badly but she never expected a car or anyone to be on the road this early and on this side of town.

"Goddamn it! Are you out of your mind?" She heard the loud roar of anger and then glanced toward the street and the dark shadow of the sheriff strutting across the front of his truck toward her.

She cringed and turned away. She was embarrassed and hurt. As if he realized that she must be injured because she was crying, he ran to her immediately.

"Oh hell, Alicia. You're hurt. Jesus, woman, you scared the crap out of me. I could have run you over. Hell, I could have killed you," he said, still sounding like he was reprimanding her.

She didn't know what scared her more—the aches and burning she felt as she wondered if something were broken and how screwed she would be considering she had no health insurance, or the intense electrifying feeling shooting through her skin as the sheriff's large hands caressed her bare arms.

Sheriff Max Gordon scared her. He was older, intimidating, and so damn powerful around this town that she knew to stay clear of him. It was only a few months back that he and his brothers acted like guardians to her while Marlena was in danger.

"I'm fine. I'm sorry. I hadn't expected anyone to be on the road. No one is usually on the road."

She turned to move and attempted to get up then cringed and moaned.

His hand landed on her knee and the other on her hip.

"Don't move. You have road burn, and dirt and scratches all over your upper thigh."

She was lying on her hip and in a very sexy position, her breasts nearly flowing from her top and her running shorts high to her groin. Even she knew she was exposing more skin than she should be with a man as sexy and intimidating as the sheriff. She felt embarrassed.

"Ah hell, baby," he said in a deep Southern tone that seemed to hit her directly in her pussy. She shivered as he held her gaze with those stunning deep brown eyes of his. The gruff on his face was even sexy and of course she was frozen in place with those big, hard, callused hands of his against her skin.

He was born and raised in South Carolina and came from a family of law enforcement officers. He had dark brown eyes that seemed to go from sweet to intense in a flash. His muscles were big, the gruff on his face an indication of how mature the man was and how masculine. Some men couldn't wear a shadow of a beard and look so lethal. The sheriff sure could. That dark expression of his as he stared at her and looked her body over had her feeling naive and stupid for nearly getting hit and having to face him. He was someone that intimidated her big time. Sheriff Max Gordon was badass and then some.

"I'll be fine. I just need to get up."

"You're not fine. I'm carrying you to the truck. I'll give you a ride back."

He went to lift her and she protested.

"No. Don't be silly. You're working, and it was partially my fault. I can get back fine."

"It was your entire fault, not partially, and on the four-mile trek back I can explain to you a little about safety precautions so you don't break your pretty little neck. Now let me get you into the truck."

She was shocked and went to protest, to tell him off, but her mouth opened and no words came out. The stinker had a sparkle in his eyes but his expression remained hard and firm as he lifted her up into his great big strong arms and held her against his chest.

She froze, unable to move, to touch him as every fiber in her body felt hot and aroused. The she prayed she didn't smell because she was so sweaty and now dirty too.

"Put your arm around my shoulder so I can get up this incline," he said. The scent of his cologne attacked her senses. The feel of his hard body beneath hers and the way his forearms felt against her skin made her pussy burn with desire. The ache she felt in her thigh and the burning sensation now that she was moving didn't seem to compare to the affect the sheriff had on her body. This wasn't good.

She was shocked and she needed to speak in order to not come across as some damsel in distress or even weak. "I can take care of myself, sheriff. Really, I'll be fine if you just set me down."

He ignored her. His expression firm. His face tense as he held her with one arm and opened the truck passenger side door with his other hand.

Even that impressed her.

When he set her down and her leg hit the leather seat she gasped.

He cursed under his breath.

"Lean to the side and toward the driver's side. You can lean on me."

He carefully closed the door and she heard him mumble something as if he were talking to someone, she wasn't sure. As he opened the driver's side door, she tried pulling back to make room for him which only aggravated her thigh more. She couldn't help but close her eyes to block the tears from falling. She'd really hurt her leg and scraped it up badly. She prayed it didn't leave a terrible scar.

In her mind she thought about Tony. He would call her a klutz, say she was unladylike for working out, and he would yell at her for damaging her perfect skin. She lifted up on her elbow and cringed again.

"Quit moving around and lay on my thigh," he ordered her.

"No. I'm fine like this."

"Alicia, quit being stubborn and do as I say. Lean on me. I'm here for you," he scolded her. She should have flipped out about the way he ordered her around, commanded her to do as he said, but then his last words lingered in her mind and played havoc with her thoughts.

Lean on me. I'm here for you. Really?

* * * *

Max was at his wits' end. He was practically shaking. He nearly ran over and killed the one woman he and his brothers set their sights on as theirs. She was stubborn, distant, quiet, shy, unreadable at times and it drove him insane. So badly he wanted to look her up in the computer system to find out anything he could about her life, but he knew better. That wasn't a way to start off a potentially promising relationship. He had trust issues. He knew that. He accepted it, but many people took offense to his hard ways and standoffish attitude. He really didn't care.

Besides, he and his brothers were tough men to deal with. They expected respect, control, and authority. Monroe and Caldwell were businessmen, entrepreneurs who were always in charge and used to it. He was the sheriff of Chance. There was a lot for them to consider.

When Alicia moved to Chance he noticed her immediately. There was an instant spark and attraction, but she didn't seem to feel the same way about him or his brothers. Then he found out through the grapevine that she left Dallas, had some bad relationship with some guy and left. It seemed to him that Alicia didn't trust easily either. Perhaps this guy, whoever he was, hurt her, broke her heart, maybe gave her the impression that men couldn't be trusted.

He and his brothers could be trusted.

He wasn't sure, but he knew other men found her attractive and were interested. He and his brothers were ready to take action. Providing protection for her a couple of months ago gave them the opportunity to start gaining that trust. Things had changed between them, but right now it seemed Alicia would rather feel pain and discomfort than lean on him for support.

He glanced at her as he put the truck into drive and headed down the road.

"Stop being so stubborn. Lay your head on my thigh and take pressure off that leg."

He gulped looking at her long, tan, sexy thigh and how she curled up on the seat. He imagined her like this on his couch, next to him and his brothers at their place, minus the cuts and bruises of course.

He licked his lower lip. Her scent was appealing, her shampoo alluring as it consumed his senses.

He gripped the steering wheel tighter the moment her head landed on his thigh.

He glanced down. So badly he would love to caress his fingers through her brown hair. Feel the softness of her skin on her cheek. He often thought about what her skin felt like to touch, to kiss, and of course explore.

His cock hardened but he wouldn't shift no matter how uncomfortable he was. If she felt his erection she might panic and jump out of the moving vehicle. He exhaled.

"We'll be in town shortly."

"In town? Why? Just drop me off at my place. I'll clean this up."

"You may need more than just basic first aid. I saw the way you landed. You could have hurt your back."

"I'm fine. I'll be okay, don't turn this into a three-ring circus."

Her comment bothered him. Especially since he just texted Monroe, who was supposed to meet him in town to discuss some investors interested in relocating their stores to Chance from Dallas. As one of the lead board members, the sheriff was careful to not exploit the town and maintain its small town feel and attraction.

"What exactly do you mean by three-ring circus? You saying something about my brothers and me?" he asked.

"No. Of course not. I mean, I just meant that if you drive into town and people see me hurt then they'll go all crazy. I saw how they treated Mary Beth last week when she tripped on the sidewalk and took a fall. They were ready to call an ambulance and bring food and pies to her house for weeks. I don't need that. I take care of myself," she said.

That was what she thought.

"Then I suppose it could be best to take you home. Do you have a first aid kit there?" he asked.

"I think Dr. Anders had one in the hall closet in the apartment. If not I'll just improvise," she said.

He took out his phone as they came to the stop sign and text the words "her house now." Hopefully Monroe would know to meet him there instead.

* * * *

Alicia eased her head up off of the sheriff's lap as the truck came to a complete stop. She inhaled one more time, loving the scent of his cologne and the hardness of his thighs as the fabric of his uniform pants tickled her cheek. She felt hot, bothered, on edge, and it amazed her and frightened her. The sheriff was mean, hard, and downright totally out of her league. She was a nobody, and he was the sheriff of Chance, a man women drooled over and talked about, wondering what type of women he liked and how many female residents of Chance he slept with. She wanted nothing to do with that.

Throw in the uniform, this patrol truck with all its gadgets and the gun, the handcuffs and superiority, and hell, she was a nervous wreck.

As she eased up she felt the achiness and downright burning pain. It was crazy. Her thigh was a complete mess. The skin was chafed back and covered in dirt and tiny stone pieces. She wanted to cry and wondered how she would get this cleaned up. She felt embarrassed having the sheriff this close to her with her short shorts on and the tank top she wore for running. She felt exposed and practically naked, but as he tried to help her up she heard the other vehicle pull up and wondered who it could be. The door slammed closed and then she gasped as the sheriff tried to help her upward from the seat.

"That hurts?" the sheriff asked and she nodded her head and tried to make the tears disappear. She prayed nothing was broken. That would be her luck. She would break bones, not know it, and then not be able to take a chance at starting her own store.

"What the hell happened?" She heard Monroe's voice just as the sheriff got her into a sitting position.

"What are you doing here?" she barked at him, unintentionally of course but it was out of her mouth before she could stop herself.

"I was supposed to meet my brother in town for a meeting. He said he was hung up and then that you were hurt. How did this happen?" Monroe asked.

"I was jogging and his truck came out of nowhere," she said.

"What? You ran from the woods right out onto the road without even looking. If it weren't for my quick reflexes and driving skills I would have hit you," the sheriff stated in anger.

"Whatever. Just help me out of your truck so you both can leave."

She eased down off the seat with the sheriff's assistance. Then Monroe placed his hand on her hip.

"That is some nasty damage. You need to clean that out thoroughly."

"I know. I will."

"Alone?" Monroe asked.

"How else?" she said and then tried to walk on her own. "Ouch, ouch, ouch, ouch," she said struggling repeatedly to make it to the walkway.

"Goddamn it. Hold on," Monroe said and scooped her up into his arms. She gasped and held onto him.

"What is with you men picking me up and carrying me? I'll get there. Just slowly."

"I'll get you there faster, and we don't mind picking you up and carrying you," he said and she felt her belly do a series of somersaults. What did that mean? She hoped they didn't think she was flirting or pretending to be hurt. Her thigh stung so badly, the tiny stones were rubbing into her cut skin.

"Key?" the sheriff asked.

"It's unlocked," she said to them.

"Unlocked. Anyone could be in there waiting for you," the sheriff said.

"You telling me that you're not doing your job and the town is unsafe?" she challenged.

He went to speak and then pointed at her.

"Lock that door for now on."

She gulped. He was so damn forceful and demanding. Why did that arouse her? She should fear that control. Then there was Monroe, who remained close-lipped as the sheriff opened the door to her apartment above the garage at Dr. Anders's place.

"Set her down on the couch," the sheriff ordered in that tone of his.

"Where did you say that first aid kit was?" he asked.

"I said I can get it and take care of it myself."

Monroe squatted down by the couch and caressed her hair from her cheek. She froze in place. Why did he have to touch her? *God, he's so good looking and he smells incredible. Shit. I probably smell. I was running and sweating. Oh God.* She was suddenly embarrassed and didn't know how she could sniff herself without making it obvious, but then the sheriff returned to the living room with other things besides a first aid kit. They were going to stay and help her. Oh God.

* * * *

Monroe took every opportunity to take in the sight of Alicia. She was so damn sexy and beautiful. The short shorts she wore were tight and small. Her thighs muscular and toned, and the tank top she wore barely confined her abundant breasts. In this position on the couch, on her side, her breasts were pouring from the top, revealing way more cleavage than he ever had the opportunity to see on Alicia.

His brother Max was getting the supplies ready to clean out the cut and ensure she didn't get an infection.

"I can do this. Really, you both don't need to waste your time. I'm sure you have better things to do," she said but Max ignored her.

"Lay still, this may sting a little."

"Max knows what he's doing, baby," Monroe said to her then placed his hand on her hip, where skin was exposed as she shifted the moment the water collided against the cuts and scrapes on her thigh.

"Ouch. Oh damn that hurts," she said and maneuvered her face into the pillow. The move caused her ass to push out nearly off the couch and gave them a perfect view of her backside.

"Stay still," Monroe told her and glanced at his brother. Max looked so serious. He probably felt responsible for her injuries. He couldn't help himself. As Max continued to wash out the wound while Alicia moaned and shivered, he caressed her arm. Her shoulder then to her hip. She was so sexy and beautiful. He thought about her all the time. When his brother texted today he thought perhaps Max made a move, Alicia accepted it, and wanted Monroe and Caldwell, too. Maybe not.

* * * *

Alicia felt her heart racing and damn it her pussy ached more than the damn cuts and scratches on her thigh. These men were so attractive, and she liked them, Caldwell, too, even though he wasn't here. God, she hoped they didn't call him to come over, too, or she was done for. They were playing with her. They had to be. They could get any woman they wanted. Why would they waste time with the likes of her?

"Thank you for doing this, but it really wasn't necessary," she said, tilting her head to the side to lock gazes with Max and Monroe.

"You never would have been able to do this on your own. You're squirming and cringing even now. I had to make sure all that dirt and bad stuff was out of it," Max said then placed his hands on her thigh and calf at each end from where the cuts and scratches began and ended. He moved her leg slightly.

"I think I got it all out. Now for the ointment," he said.

She turned toward him. "You don't have to do that. I can get it," she said, taking in the sight of his uniform, the badge, and that older, more seasoned expression he always had. She was angering him. He was complicated. Her life was way too complicated already.

She felt the hand on her shoulder then fingers touch her chin and tilt it upward. Her eyes locked gazes with Monroe.

"It's our responsibility to protect you and watch out for you. We don't want to ever see you hurt, or in pain. Got that?" he asked.

Her core tightened and in her mind she wished she were different, stronger, capable of having men like Monroe, Caldwell, and Max, but she wasn't. She was weak, palpable to the point where their control, their good looks, their attraction she felt for them would overrule her rational mind and make her succumb to hurt and sadness once again. Like the books she read all said. *You must first admit to the problem, agree that you have a problem before you can make changes to alleviate the problem and make it disappear.* She'd been trying to do that for the better part of a year now. No such luck.

"I am not your responsibility. It isn't your job to protect me and watch over me. You had to do that for a week while Marlena was in danger. We're months past that. Listen, I'm not going to argue with you. I appreciate the help with this, but I think I'll be okay."

She felt Max press the ointment to her raw skin and she flinched. "Oh God," she whispered.

"Easy, baby. I know it burns. I'll be quick," Max said. The fact that he called her "baby" was one thing, but the way it made her feel was completely another. Her pussy clenched, her breasts felt full, and she wished for things she stopped wishing for once Tony screwed her over.

Monroe stood up and walked toward the wall with her displays of stained glass panels she made. Then he looked at the one she was working on. A custom order.

"These are amazing, Alicia. You should open up your own storefront."

Max wiped his hands after he closed up the tube.

"I don't know. It's risky."

Monroe turned toward her.

"But you're doing well, selling on eBay?" he asked.

"I'm doing very well there."

"Then you should consider opening up a small storefront. You can do custom orders and then random sales on eBay still."

"I've thought about it."

"You go to the new construction site on the edge of town a lot. You considering renting one of the storefronts there?" Max asked her and she saw Monroe's eyes light up.

"I don't think so. I mean, maybe. I don't know, why?" she asked and then turned to sit up, feeling the effects of the ointment kick in.

"This is amazing work. You're very talented," Max told her then walked out of the room to the bathroom to wash his hands she assumed as she heard the water start a few seconds after he disappeared.

"Is that what you were doing? You were checking out the construction site?" Monroe asked her.

"I like going there and see it improve every day. It's going to be a prime location," she said as she placed her hands on her lap.

"I heard that they sold six out of the twelve storefronts already. If you're considering it, let Caldwell and me know. We're friends with the guy building them."

"Oh, well like I said, I'm not sure I'm ready for that. I mean I would love to. Don't get me wrong, but I don't know if I want to take the financial risk. It's a lot to consider."

"Hey, your stuff is great. If you don't want to take it all on yourself, you could find a partner, or someone who supports your work that's willing to back you financially."

"And if it fails, then what? I owe that person my life?"

"No, there are ways to protect both parties. If you're interested, talk to Caldwell or myself. We know people," he told her and she nodded her head as she took in the sight of Monroe. He wore dress pants, a pair of cowboy boots peeked out from the hem on his ankles, and he wore a blue button-down shirt, no tie. He looked good. He looked classy.

She heard him clear his throat and then cross his arms in front of his chest.

"The place looks good. You're a neat freak huh?" he asked.

"I wouldn't say that. You haven't been in her bathroom," Max said and then winked at Monroe.

"What's wrong with my bathroom?" she asked and tried to stand up as she thought about how she might have left it this morning. She was a bit of a neat freak. She was always cleaning. In fact, she cleaned the bathroom this morning.

Then she remembered how she washed out some bras and thong panties to hang on the line she made in the bathroom shower. Oh God. He saw them. The sheriff saw her panties hanging in there.

Alicia felt her cheeks warm and she cleared her throat.

"So, thanks again for the help."

She grunted as she got up and Max reached for her to help her.

"I'm fine."

He held her gaze. His dark brown eyes bore into hers.

"You're more than fine, Alicia. You're perfect."

She didn't know why he said that and she didn't want to ask, but didn't get the chance. He excused himself and said he needed to get back to work.

"Now you be sure to cover that up and reapply the ointment. I'll check in on you later."

"That won't be necessary. I have work to do."

"I'll text you."

She wondered how he would do that since she never gave out her cell number, and then it hit her. He was the sheriff, he could find out anything. She thought about Tony and how he sold the company they had right out from underneath her and how he cheated on her and basically used her. The sheriff could know already and he and his brothers could be looking to do the same thing.

"Alicia." She heard her name and there was Monroe.

"Are you okay?" he asked, placing his hands on her shoulders.

She shook them off and stepped back, ignoring the ache.

"Please leave. I'll be fine." She looked toward the sheriff. "Don't call me or text me. I'll take care of myself, thank you."

She thought Max might challenge her but instead he looked perplexed and he winked before he opened the door and indicated he was waiting on Monroe to leave with him.

Monroe smiled.

"You take care of that leg and be sure to call me about the storefront. We can make it happen together."

The door closed and she sighed feeling the tears in her eyes.

I bet you could. You and your two brothers would use me, play with my emotions and truly destroy any bit of self-confidence I may have left somewhere inside of me. You're all hot and sexy, but no thank you. I'm destined for loneliness. That's the way it has to be.

Chapter 2

"I don't think she's coming," Max said as he stood in the kitchen along with his brothers. He had a feeling Alicia would change her mind despite how excited Caldwell was about getting her over here for a project. He didn't think it was such a great idea since Alicia was so shy and seemed timid when it came to them. It felt like he got her here under false pretenses and that could only mean disaster.

"She'll come here, despite her injury. Even though she seems fearful of us she is still professional. That's one of the qualities I personally find endearing," Caldwell replied.

"I hope her leg is okay," Monroe said as they heard the doorbell ring.

"Holy shit. She's here," Monroe added and Caldwell hurried down the hallway to the door.

Max and Monroe followed and as Caldwell opened the door there stood Alicia looking incredible as usual.

She pushed the strand of hair behind her ear and shyly looked up at Caldwell.

"Sorry I'm late, my car wouldn't start."

Caldwell looked past her and Max felt concerned.

"Maybe you should get that checked out?" Monroe said as he joined them by the front door.

She looked over her shoulder toward her car. "That's okay. It's been doing that for a while."

"Well then you should definitely get it checked out. The last thing you need is to be stuck on the side of the road somewhere all alone," Max said to her, instantly hoping she heeded his advice. He couldn't help but to think of all the bad things that could happen to a beautiful woman like Alicia stuck on the side of the road in the middle of nowhere.

"It will be fine," she said, looking at Max as if he upset her.

"Come on inside. Welcome to our home," Caldwell interrupted and she smiled and entered.

Max felt his gut clench. She was so petite compared to the three of them it made him feel protective as usual.

"This is so big, and the ceilings are so high," she told them as she walked around and took in the sight.

"We're tall men. Always hated walking into places and having to duck between every doorway," Monroe told her.

She nodded her head.

"I wouldn't know how that feels," she said and Monroe smiled.

Max looked her over. "How is your thigh? You taking good care of it? Applying the ointment?" he asked.

She swallowed hard and looked up at him with an expression that warned him to be patient with her. She was a timid thing.

"Yes, sheriff. It still hurts a bit but I'll be fine," she said and he raised one of his eyebrows up at her but before he could tell her to call him Max, his brother interrupted.

"Can I get you something to drink?" Monroe asked.

"No, thank you. If you would like to show me the wine cellar and this window you want me to see, that would be great and I can get out of your hair in no time."

"You're not in our hair. It's nice to have you here," Caldwell said and she pulled her bottom lip between her teeth and lowered her head.

Max cleared his throat.

"It's this way," Max said and motioned with his hand for her to follow him.

He could smell her perfume and he hoped the hallway, their house, still smelled of it when she left so he could enjoy it some more.

He opened the door and they headed down the stairs. She seemed hesitant to follow them into the basement. He couldn't blame her.

As soon as the cellar came into sight he heard Alicia sigh.

"Oh my, this is stunning, and so big," she said as she moved around the room and toward the window.

"That's a lot of wine bottles you have in here," she said, looking at the custom-made wine racks and tasting table. Her hands glided along the wood and he gulped down his own thoughts of those hands on his body. Touching him. Exploring him. No woman ever made Max feel this way. Not by a long shot. In fact, most women would have already been in their bed by now, but Alicia was different. She was the first woman they wanted to take their time with. Although watching her in the sexy skirt, her tanned legs down to her small heeled sandals and manicured toes, then up her flat belly to her well-endowed breasts was causing his heart to race. Was it hot in here? He pulled the collar from his neck and tried to ease the sensations. She made him nervous, uneasy, and out of sorts. He didn't like the feeling. It made him desperate to end this and just kiss her already.

"Over eight hundred bottles can be stored on the racks alone, never mind the special cellar below," Monroe said.

"A special cellar?" she asked.

Max smiled as he crossed his arms in front of his chest.

"Here we go. Caldwell and Monroe spared no expense when it came to this project."

"Come over here, Alicia, and I'll show you," Monroe said and took her by her elbow. Max watched her pull her bottom lip between her teeth and hesitate, but she went with him. Her knee-length flair skirt tapped against her knees.

"Can you reach up and grab me that statue of the wine maker? I want to show you something," he said. When Alicia reached for the statue and pulled back, the door began to open from behind the bookcase.

She stepped back and Monroe pressed up against her as he clutched her shoulders.

"Don't be afraid."

"Yeah, it's not quite a dungeon," Max teased.

"A dungeon. I don't think so," she said and turned as if she were going to leave. Monroe gave Max a dirty look as he grabbed her hand.

"Please, don't listen to him, he's trying to get a rile out of you. It's safe and even cool. I promise."

As they headed inside, the small hallway wound to the right and Monroe hit the switch on the wall. Immediately the inner room illuminated and Alicia gasped and placed her hands together moving closer.

"Oh my God, Monroe, this is incredible," she said and entered the private wine-tasting room decorated in Tuscan colors and a vintage feel. There was raised grape wall paint surrounding the arched doorway to the room and then authentic barrels of wine and some wrought iron cabinets that encased expensive wine bottles being aged for the right occasion and Alicia looked impressed.

"Do you like it?" Caldwell asked, joining them.

"Like it? Are you kidding me? I've never seen anything like this before. I'm very impressed. Do you do tastings down here during parties?" she asked, letting her hand slide along the marble counter and tasting area, then against the wood that a local wood-making artist created just for the room.

"Only a select few people have seen this room. Monroe likes to escape down here when he's overstressed," Max told her.

"Hmm. That must be nice to have a place to go to in order to separate from the stress. Some low lights or candles, a nice glass of wine and some—"

The sound of Italian music began to play softly in the background. Max chuckled.

Alicia looked so beautiful and being in this enclosed space sent his body into such a need. Max wanted to hold her in his arms. He wanted to touch her. Hell, he wanted to claim her as their woman and bypass all this courting stuff, but his brothers and him agreed to ease her into a relationship. They needed to gain her trust and what better way than to have her work here.

"So what do you think about the window and how we have everything set up? Any ideas come to mind for it?" Monroe asked as Caldwell led them out of the secret cellar and back into the main cellar. She watched as the bookcase moved back into place.

She walked over toward the window and then back toward Monroe and Caldwell.

"You could go as extreme as you want here. I don't know what your budget is for the job but let me think of a few ideas and get back to you. Traditionally speaking, a set of grapes clustered between a few bottles of wine that say Bordeaux, Chardonnay, and Cabernet or Pinot noir would look great. The word winery at the top, or maybe even some scene from Italy like a vineyard and people working the fields? There are lots of options," she told them and then she took a notebook from her bag and then jotted some things down.

"Could I take a picture of this area?" she asked.

"Sure thing. Whatever you need. Oh, and there's really no budget. We want something unique and we love your work," Monroe told her.

"Thank you, Monroe. I appreciate the vote of confidence. I'm certain I can come up with something the three of you will love."

She took a few different pictures showcasing each angle and then wrote some more notes. Max watched as she pulled out a tape measurer and measured the window, needing Monroe's help to hold the tape at one end.

"You really love doing this stuff huh, Alicia?" Caldwell asked her.

"Oh yes. I love creating custom designs for people. It's harder to recreate designs I've already made when people order online. I like the pieces to truly be unique but people have ideas in their heads and they are paying me. I try to get them exactly what they've ordered but sometimes my creativity sends me a little different way and thank God no one has complained or pulled out of an order," she told them.

"You should open up your own store and sell the things you create and love to do. Then you won't have to worry about recreating the same identical things for people. You can be completely in charge," Monroe suggested.

She took a deep breath and exhaled.

"I would love to but I honestly don't know if I can handle it on my own. I get so caught up in the creative part and the designing and making things that the business end would suffer."

"You could always have a partner, someone who could assist you with the business aspect, marketing, advertising and all," Monroe suggested.

"That in itself is a risk," she said to them.

"Not with the right partner. If you're really interested in pursuing a storefront, let me know and I would be willing to help you."

"Oh God, Monroe, I couldn't ask that of you. You hardly know me."

"Well, my brothers and I are working on getting to know you, but I see your determination and your love of this art. Why don't you mull it over while you're working here and maybe we could come up with a deal? One that won't make you feel like if anything went wrong we could lose this comfortable relationship and friendship we currently have?"

Max watched her hesitate and Monroe pushed. "Come on. I promise to come up with something you'll feel comfortable with, and by the time you're done working here and finishing the mosaic, you'll know my brothers and I a lot better and you'll feel comfortable. Come on," he pushed.

"No promises but I guess so," she replied then pulled her bottom lip between her teeth. Max saw the delight on Monroe's face and Caldwell didn't hide his smile as he stood by the window, arms crossed, and watched Alicia. She turned around and looked at the window again and then the wine cellar before writing some things down in her notebook. She looked comfortable and happy in her art and designing. Now he understood at least something that brought a smile, a glow into her eyes. Hopefully this didn't backfire on them.

"Great, now how about something to eat? We prepared some food earlier."

"That wasn't necessary. I thought I was just stopping in. I don't want to intrude on your plans, if any."

"Our plan was to go over some ideas for the window. So let's head upstairs, grab some wine and snacks, and go over it again. I want to hear your ideas and how you perceive that window to be done," Monroe said and she nodded her head and they headed upstairs. Max couldn't help but feel a bit confident about the way things were going. If they played their cards right, Alicia would be their woman and they would focus on getting to know her in no time. Maybe Monroe's plan would work after all?

* * * *

Initially Alicia felt pretty damn nervous being in the kitchen with Max, Caldwell, and Monroe. Soon they were joking around with one another and making her feel pretty comfortable. She found out that Max was investigating a local crime where someone was breaking into unlocked vehicles and stealing any change or sellable items. He felt that the culprits were teenagers and more than likely not from Chance. He warned her about locking her doors and she nodded in agreement but knew she would leave the door unlocked. It was easier than having to carry a key when she went jogging. She felt a bit guilty because she left the house today and left the doors unlocked, too. Maybe she should listen to his advice?

"What other businesses are you involved in right now?" she asked Monroe. He glanced at his brother Caldwell. Caldwell's eyes were the deepest blue she had ever seen. She couldn't help but to stare at him until Monroe cleared his throat. Caldwell licked his lower lip as he held her gaze and once again she felt out of their league. She wasn't used to flirting or being flirted with. The last year she spent trying to gain control of her life and her emotions instead of crying herself to sleep every night. She didn't need more heartbreak.

"Currently we have about four businesses we own. One we help operate. It's in Dallas. It's one of the major dance halls around town. We own two strip malls in San Antonio, one in New York," Monroe explained.

"We have some smaller shops we own and help support like we mentioned doing for you," Caldwell said.

She pulled her bottom lip between her teeth.

"I haven't said yes to the help. I'm not sure I really need it."

"So you have the money to buy the storefront?" Monroe asked her.

"No. I have the money to rent it. Owning it would be even riskier."

"But when your business does well, whoever owns it gains a lot of control over you and your business. They can raise the rates, the rent. They can build up or break down your business. That's a risk you shouldn't take," Monroe told her.

"But I don't have that kind of money to buy out a building," she said, feeling discouraged. What Monroe said made sense. Once again someone would have control over her and her business. They could close the store on her even if she were successful. Then what?

He must have noticed the panic on her face. Max cleared his throat.

"There are other options. How much is Dwyer selling the storefronts for Caldwell?" Max asked.

"Sixty thousand."

"Sixty thousand? Oh God," she said and placed her hand over her belly. She instantly felt sick. The heat hit her cheeks and she felt faint. Then someone took her hand and patted it. Caldwell.

"Relax. This is why we suggested letting us go into this as partners with you. No stress or worry about being taken over or losing the storefront. Plus we know Dwyer. We can probably get that number down especially if we buy more than one storefront," Caldwell said to her.

"More than one storefront? Why?" she asked.

"Well, that location is prime. There are a few different ideas we had about developing them into something this town could really use. Not sure what yet, but it would be wise to invest in one or two of the stores. How much space do you think you'll need for the studio?" Monroe asked.

"Oh God, I don't know. I really don't even know how big the storefronts are."

"Well, have you been into the Alexa's boutique and hat store in Chance in the center of town?" Monroe asked her.

"Yes."

"Okay so the storefronts Dwyer is building with Ferguson construction on the strip are just a little bigger than that. I think it would be more than enough room for you to display your artwork and also create your masterpieces while people watch," Monroe said.

"People watching me? Oh no. I don't like the sound of that. I would feel embarrassed and pressured. I need my music and sometimes just silence."

"It was just a thought. We'll work it all out. Your art sells itself."

"I don't know about that, Monroe. It's tough when you're not known," she told him, lowering her head.

"Let us worry about that. You worry about creating those masterpieces," Monroe said.

"I really need to think this through."

"Then think for the next week while you start our project here. By next week or so they'll only be a few of the storefronts left for sale. You'll take our advice on which location, won't you?" Monroe asked.

She felt pressured and unsure. Were they being sincere or would they turn out to be like Tony? Out for themselves.

"I said, I need to think about it. I'll let you know," she said.

"Great. Now, what do you like to do when you're not working in your studio or running out in front of Sheriff patrol trucks?" Caldwell teased.

She felt her cheeks warm.

"That wasn't entirely my fault."

"No?" Max asked, his arms crossed in front of his wide chest, giving her that intimidating stare down.

"I didn't think so. But no worries, Max. I learned my lesson. Every time I move around this ache in my thigh reminds me," she said and Max's expression changed to concern. He reached out under her chair and pulled it toward him. She grabbed onto the sides.

Her thighs were now between his large, splayed thighs as he sat in the chair.

"Let me take a look to be sure it's healing okay," he said, with both his hands on her knees. He used his thumbs to caress her skin and she felt flushed, excited, scared, and couldn't speak. Her breasts tingled and she gripped the chair.

"I'm okay," she said.

He slowly pushed the one side of her skirt upward.

"Jesus, Alicia," Caldwell said and knelt down next to her chair. He placed his hand on her chair as Max eased the skirt higher.

Any further and she would be showing off her hip bone and panties.

"Alicia, you need to be more careful," Caldwell reprimanded her as he placed his hands on her shoulders from behind her chair and leaned over looking at her thigh. With three sets of sexy eyes on her she panicked. She shoved her skirt down and pushed up and out of the chair. She nearly lost her balance but Max grabbed her hips as he stood. He towered over her.

"Sweetheart, don't be scared of us. We'd never hurt you."

"Don't say things like that to me."

"Why not? It's true. Don't you believe me?" he asked. She shook her head.

"I need to go."

"Wait," Monroe said and took her hand.

"I'll walk you out. We'll make plans for designs on the window. I'll give you my contact info. E-mail, phone number, and we can go over designs together. I can relay the info to my brothers. Maybe you can start in a couple of days? If that's good for you of course," Monroe said as he escorted her from the kitchen.

She glanced over her shoulder at Max and Caldwell, who just stared at her. Max looked pissed off. He ran his fingers through his hair and exhaled. She quickly turned around and headed toward the front door with Monroe. Something was going on here, but what, exactly?

* * * *

"Oh my God we were so close. I thought you were going to kiss her, Max," Caldwell said to his brother once Monroe and Alicia exited the house.

Max ran his fingers through his hair. Caldwell thought he looked unraveled and angry.

"Goddamn it I wanted to. I'm not used to this sidestepping, waiting shit. Most women would be throwing themselves at us, but not Alicia. I swear when she looks at me sometimes I think she sees a monster," Max said in frustration.

"I don't think she sees you as a monster as much as an intimidating, lawful figure. You don't realize the kind of reputation you have around Chance, Max."

"My reputation? Shit, I've never worried about any of that. Hell, our fathers never did either if you recall."

Caldwell chuckled as he crossed his arms and leaned back against the counter. Max was right.

"Shit, Brook Gordon still scares the shit out of people when he shows his face in Chance."

Max chuckled. "What about you? You're more like Walt than Monroe and I."

"I'd rather be more like Walt, who holds back his anger, then when pushed over the edge roars like a lion. You're the one royally screwed with a combined personality of Colonel, Brook, and Sianne."

"Hey, I'll tell Mom you said that next time she calls."

"Ha, she knows you're just like her. The woman's quiet as can be and when the fathers ruffle her feathers all hell breaks loose. Come to think of it, I wonder if that's why we like Alicia so much. She does kind of remind me of Mom. God, if they come visiting, what will they think of Alicia?"

"I think Mom will love her and the dads, too. Especially if she's shy and timid. Mom will have us boosting Alicia's self-confidence and helping her to feel loved and protected."

"Well, don't go making the call to Mom and the dads yet. I think we might have scared Alicia a little bit, or intimidated her," Monroe added to the conversation as he entered the room. He leaned one hand on the counter and kept the other on his hip.

"She's a tough one to read. I swear I think someone hurt her or let her down big time. Do we know if she has any family? Any relatives alive?" Monroe asked.

"I thought we discussed not snooping around," Max said to him.

"I don't know if it's really snooping."

Caldwell laughed at Monroe.

"Mr. Cool and Calm is feeling a bit out of control I see. We need to be respectful. We'll get to know her and gain her trust when she's working here. Stay calm."

"Stay calm? How the hell can you stay so calm when she smells so good, looks so good, and damn it I bet feels so good to hold?" Monroe asked.

"Patience, Monroe. Remember what our mamma always said, about good things coming to those who wait and patience pays off in the end."

"Well can we fast forward through the bullshit and make Alicia ours already? This is fucking torture," Monroe added.

"Well, when did she say she could start? That's how we'll know how long this torture might be lasting," Caldwell asked.

"In a couple of days."

"Well then, let's have a beer and make a toast to getting through this so we can claim our woman and start working on becoming a family. God knows Mamma's been hinting about grandkids and settling down. She'll love that we're considering it sooner than later," Max said.

"Mamma finds out about Alicia, she'll show up here and try to help," Monroe added and all three chuckled.

"Then God help us we can get through to Alicia and prove our intentions are noble. Otherwise they'll be hell to pay and Sianne Gordon is not the kind of woman we need to make angry," Caldwell added and they laughed as Max grabbed the beers.

Chapter 3

"Please, Alvin, I'm fine. I've just been really busy with work," Alicia said into the phone as she tried to get ready to meet Max, Caldwell, and Monroe at their house with the final idea for the window in their winery. She'd taken a couple of extra days to pull together a small replica of her idea on a stained glass piece. She figured if they liked it she would give it to them to use somewhere else in their house.

"Too busy to call me back? To talk to Tony? I doubt it. Unless you haven't told me about some other fabulous job you got where you're making a lot of money," he snapped at her. She felt the tears reach her eyes. She hated when he got this way. He seemed to focus more and more on himself and his wants than hers. Plus the fact that he really believed she would be his financial savior. She didn't need men like this in her life.

She used the special cleaner to shine up the 16 x 18 stained glass piece. It looked stunning and she hoped they liked it.

"Are you listening to me?" Alvin raised his voice.

"Yes. Of course I am but I need to get going."

"Where? It's nearly seven."

"I have an appointment."

"At night? With whom? It isn't a date is it?"

"No. It's business."

"With male or female?"

"With none of your business."

Alvin was silent.

"Don't go making some huge mistake. Tony still wants you after everything, even the accusations that he cheated on you."

"He did cheat on me."

"You were upset about losing the business. Your poor decisions caused that. It's no wonder you made up the lies about Tony having affairs and seeing other women. He would never do that to you. Don't you be stupid now and start fucking a bunch of guys. Tony will never take back used goods."

"I'm not used goods."

"You slept with Tony before you were even married. Do you know what Mom and Dad would have done?"

"No, I don't because I hardly knew them anyway. Besides, I'm not involved with anyone. Tony broke my heart in case you didn't realize that."

Her brother was silent.

"It was your fault, not his. Get it together, because when he wants to take you back you won't want to have any regrets."

God, he frustrated her so much. She was sick and tired of this same conversation. He feared she would find another man, a boyfriend, a husband, and all his wants would diminish and Alvin would have to support himself. She took a deep breath. *My God what would he do if he knew about the ménage relationships running rampant in Chance?* Or if he knew she was attracted to three brothers. Real men who would probably knock Alvin and Tony out with one punch? *I can't like three men. I wasn't even able to keep one man from cheating on me. The Gordon brothers would use me and indeed I would be used property.*

Damn Alvin! Why does he always make me feel like shit?

She didn't need a nervous breakdown now when she had this huge job starting in another day. That was if the Gordon brothers liked her idea. She was having second thoughts. She was feeling like she wasn't good enough. Tony and Alvin did this to her. They made her feel like without them making decisions for her she would screw up.

She swallowed hard and tried to keep the tears at bay as Alvin demanded to know where she was going and who she was meeting.

"I'm doing a big job for some friends in town. It's a large window in their wine cellar."

"Who are they?"

"The sheriff and his…family. Very nice people and he loves my work so I'm doing this private project for them."

"Well don't forget to keep in touch and call Tony. He said he's planning on visiting you and misses you."

"I don't want him coming here. It's none of his business what I'm doing."

"Then be sure to call him and me back immediately when we call. Otherwise he will check in on you. Remember, no other man will want you since you gave it up to Tony. If he wants you back, you'd better accept it. Otherwise there'll never be a man out there who will respect you, want you, and honestly love you." He disconnected the call and Alicia slammed the phone down.

"I hate you. I hate both of you and wish you would just leave me alone."

The tears rolled down her cheeks and she tried unsuccessfully to wipe them away. She would be late to the Gordon men's home. She needed to dry out first.

* * * *

"Maybe she changed her mind. Maybe you pushed too much, Monroe," Max said to his brother as he stood in the kitchen looking impatient.

"Nonsense. She said she came up with an idea and wanted to present it to us. I can't wait to see what drawings she came up with," Monroe said.

They heard the doorbell ring and Caldwell headed toward it. "I'll get it." Monroe and Max headed toward it, too.

The second Monroe saw her face he could see that something was wrong. She said a quick hello and walked in carrying a large box.

"Is everything okay?" he asked her. She nodded.

"Just fine. Let's head into the kitchen so I can show you my idea," she said but her voice cracked and she seemed sad. He glanced at Max and Caldwell, who appeared to have noticed as well.

Monroe took in the sight of her as she laid the box onto the table and began to unwrap the packaging. She looked good. She wore a pair of capris in beige and a matching tan-and-white tank blouse that showed off her sun-kissed skin and toned arms. Her hair was pulled up into a fancy style and appeared to be held up by one lone clip in white. She looked very pretty.

"So, this is my idea," she said and undid the box. She lifted the piece but before she even had it out of the box and in the light of the kitchen he loved it.

"Oh my God, Alicia. You made that?" he asked and moved closer.

"Holy cow that is stunning," Caldwell said and Max walked closer. He eyed over the Tuscan scene, a sunset over a large vineyard. To the bottom right was a house, similar to their own with a table and four chairs. On the table were a bottle of red wine, a bottle of white wine, and four glasses, plus a platter of cheeses and grapes in green purple and red. The detail was amazing.

Max placed his hands on her shoulders.

"It's stunning. I've never seen anything like it. You can create this on the window downstairs?" he asked, seeming stunned at her capabilities. There were tears in her eyes as she nodded her head. She stared at the stained glass creation as if analyzing her own work. When she spoke he heard her own criticism of the piece.

"If you don't like certain aspects of it I understand and can tweak them. Perhaps you don't like the house or the wine-tasting table. Or maybe the sunset behind the vineyard."

"Are you kidding me? This is more than we expected. This is perfection," Monroe told her.

"You're truly talented, Alicia. I'm so impressed," Max added and gave her shoulders a squeeze.

Monroe saw the tears in her eyes and she cleared her throat and stepped from the table, giving them a better amount of space to look at the piece. And look they did, at every detail and at her ability to be so meticulous.

"Are you sure this is what you had in mind?" she asked, standing to the side with her hands clasped in front of her.

"Baby, it looks incredible. It's perfect. You're amazing," Caldwell told her and she chuckled, her cheeks turning a shade of pink.

"Now make this night even more perfect and tell me you made a decision about us backing you financially for your own shop and studio where you can sell this stuff and promote your talent," Monroe said.

"God, Monroe, I'm just not certain. You make me feel like it's possible."

"It is possible. You can trust us," he said and walked closer to her.

She shook her head.

"I don't want to be in debt to you. I don't want to ruin this friendship or business relationship. What if things go wrong? What if people don't buy my work and don't like it?"

"Honey, they already love your pieces on eBay. They'll love it here in Chance and elsewhere. We know what we're doing. We don't back anyone who we don't believe in or support or think won't be successful," Caldwell added.

"We'll see. I need a little more time."

"Okay, but know that we believe in your capabilities and talent," Monroe told her.

"Who wouldn't, after seeing this piece alone?" Max said, holding her gaze.

"How about a glass of wine and a look at what this piece appears like over the window downstairs?" Monroe suggested. He watched her expression change and she still looked kind of sad.

"Sure. That's a great idea. Then you can make the final decision and I can start tomorrow."

"Excellent," Caldwell added and they headed down to the wine cellar with the glass piece in hand.

* * * *

Alicia was feeling a bit better. She had an easy time talking to Monroe and Caldwell, and was beginning to get used to Max's hard expressions. He seemed very nice, too, and she was glad to become friends with them, but she was still uncertain about the business deal.

"I appreciate your compliments. I think I would have been shattered if you disliked my ideas. I have a personal attachment to each piece I make and sometimes I need a little transition time to give it away. But this one I just felt the three of you would love. I'm glad that you're happy with it and don't hate it as I feared. It would have been the perfect ending to a horrible day," she said as she took another sip of wine. She didn't know much about wine, but she did have her favorite white and red.

"What do you mean a horrible day? Did something happen?" Monroe asked her as they sat around the small wine-tasting table in front of the window.

"Well, it was just a hard one," she said and thought about her brother and the way he acted.

"Anything we could help you with? You know, maybe talk about to get off your chest," Caldwell suggested.

She shook her head.

"We just became friends and I'm also working for you now so it probably wouldn't be a great idea to spill my guts."

"Why not? Like you said, we're friends now," Caldwell said.

She smiled. "You're sweet, and I appreciate that. I think we should keep this professional. After all, you've given me an opportunity to showcase my work and even offered to back me financially for the store. I think we have some details to work out but keeping it strictly business is a great idea. I won't feel so vulnerable or at risk emotionally. I've had some bad experiences in my life that I don't want to repeat."

"We've all had bad experiences. Those are what make us stronger," Monroe told her.

"You're amazing, Monroe. I understand why you guys are so successful in business and in life. You have it all together. You're strong, empowered, and confident."

"You don't see yourself as confident?" Max asked her.

She leaned back in the chair.

"I probably shouldn't be telling you this, but I'm not a confident person. I'm very critical of myself and well, past experiences have weakened that confidence in me. But your compliments tonight and the fact that you still want to back me in opening a store really mean a lot to me. I'm glad we're friends, and that there's no other pressure for anything else but business. It's what I need right now. People who believe in my art and really are supportive. So, how about I start this project here tomorrow and then by Friday we can talk details to a possible business arrangement?" she asked but all three men seemed different. They seemed sad or maybe shocked. She wasn't certain but Monroe smiled wide.

"We're glad to help out. We'll definitely talk business by Friday. In the meantime we should get you a key so you can get in and out of here if we're stuck at work or need to leave for early meetings."

"Oh, are you sure? I mean you don't really know me that well," she said.

"As long as you lock up when you leave we don't mind at all," Max teased and she chuckled. Maybe things were finally looking up after all?

* * * *

Monroe stood in shock just like his brothers once Alicia left. He felt numb and totally out of sorts. His brothers obviously felt the same way, too.

"Well, you're idea backfired on us. She thinks we want to be her best friends. She thinks we're only into her for business reasons. I told you this was going to get screwed up. We should have just focused on getting to know her here on the job and not trying to help her financially as you suggested Monroe. Why can't we just tell her how we feel?" Caldwell asked.

"I'm thinking okay. The last thing I expected was for her to think of us as friends and nothing else. It will work out. Maybe this is for the better," Monroe said.

"For the better, huh? How the hell are we supposed to be around her and not want to touch her, kiss her, and get to know her?" Max asked.

"We just need to do things a little differently so she feels safe and learns to trust us. So we learn about her as friends. We make her feel comfortable and when the time is right we can come clean and be honest about our feelings."

"How the hell long will that take?" Max asked.

"As long as it does. She's special and we're in this for the long haul so I say it's worth it. She's worth it don't you think?"

"Of course, but this is going to be torture," Caldwell said as he downed another sip of wine.

"She'll be here in our home getting to know each of us. That will work in our favor if she is attracted to the three of us."

"God I hope so, Monroe, because the more I'm around her the stronger my feelings get for her," Caldwell said.

"It will work out fine. Let's give her a chance to realize that she likes us, too, and as more than just friends. After all, this will give each of us time to make sure that she's the one for us. How else would we know for sure?"

"By kissing her and holding her in our arms, that's how," Max said in frustration and Caldwell mumbled in agreement. Monroe chuckled.

"Well, like everything else we'll be tortured together. Here's to our pursuit of happiness and landing a very special woman to make ours." Monroe raised his glass and so did his brothers, toasting Alicia and what they hoped was yet to come.

Chapter 4

"So how is it really going working for the Gordon men?" Marlena asked Alicia as they sat on the back porch at Marlena's cottage.

Alicia sighed. "It's going very well. They're really nice and respectful."

Marlena chuckled.

"Nice and respectful? Hmm."

"What?" Alicia asked and Marlena chuckled.

"You like them."

"What's not to like? They're gorgeous, manly, courteous, and caring. Hell, they seem perfect."

"That's wonderful so when are you going to make a move?"

"Make a move? Hello? I'm not going to do any such thing."

"Why the heck not? They like you, you like them, there's not much more to figure out," Marlena said, feeling surprised that Alicia was acting this way. She knew her friend had been hurt before.

"What gives?" Marlena pushed.

Alicia pushed up off the chair and stood. She looked out toward the lake in the distance. Marlena could see her gripping the wooden railing. Something was holding Alicia back.

"Monroe and Caldwell offered to back me financially to open my own storefront in the new strip on the edge of town."

"That's wonderful. You said you didn't want to use all your savings and risk sinking in the business and then being left with nothing. This makes it less risky."

Alicia turned to look at Marlena.

"It's more risky."

"Why is that?"

"Because, I was in business with my ex, Tony. We talked about doing all these things and the business was doing great. Then suddenly he sold everything out from underneath me. He cheated on me, used me, and left me with nothing but what money I had stashed away in a savings he didn't know about."

"They're not him."

"How do you know they aren't? They have reputations around town. Monroe and Caldwell are known as ladies men with lots of money and whom are very successful. They could have their choice of women whenever they want them. The sheriff? Well there are bets going around about how many women in Chance he's slept with. Not exactly commitment material to me. I don't need another man and in this case, men, using me and leaving me to get out of debt and be miserable once again. I can't trust them."

"Oh, Alicia, I think you have it all wrong. I can understand your fears about the business thing. If you're that adamant about getting their help then do it on your own."

"It's a lot of money. It won't leave me much for advertising costs and then a mortgage, if I can even get one. I'm not exactly showing consistent income and a steady job. What bank would give me a loan?"

"Have you discussed particulars with Monroe and Caldwell? Maybe there's a way they could hold the mortgage for you and you would pay them like they were a bank?"

"But it still gives them control over me. Tony broke my heart. I thought I loved him and that he loved me. But he used me and til this day he has this control over me."

"What do you mean? He's still calling you, putting you down and you're listening to him?" Marlena asked. She was shocked.

"He's my brother's best friend. Which by the way, Alvin does not think Tony can do any wrong. I told you guys how my own brother continuously takes Tony's side. How he even wants me to get back together with Tony so he can get financial assistance. I wouldn't put him past coming here and checking up on me to make sure I'm not involved with anyone. Do you know what he would do if he came to Chance and saw the types of relationships around here?"

"Damn, they really are no good weasels.."

"Tell me about it," Alicia said and lowered her head and closed her eyes. Marlena stood up and placed her hand on her shoulder.

"Okay, tell me everything from start to present. All about the business and the relationship with Tony and where your brother plays a role in it all. Then let's see if we can figure this out together. I still think that Monroe, Max, and Caldwell are nothing like this Tony guy or your brother Alvin. But, you need to feel confident and safe. This is a big deal and you don't need another setback financially or emotionally. Come on. Let's sit down and talk this out. I'm sure we can come up with something."

They sat back down and Alicia exhaled.

"Can I just ask you something?" Marlena asked.

"Go ahead."

"Do you like them? Monroe, Caldwell, and Max?"

Alicia pulled her bottom lip between her teeth and nodded her head. Marlena could see the tears in her eyes. She reached over and covered her hand with hers.

"Awe, honey. Is it just the financial thing that's holding you back or this guy Tony and your brother?"

"All of the above. I don't want to be betrayed ever again. I don't want to worry about Tony and Alvin showing up and pushing me to be what they want me to be."

"Then you need to stand up for yourself. You need to decide what you want."

"That's more easily said than done. You don't know Tony. He can be persuasive when he wants something."

"He sounds like a bully to me."

Marlena listened as Alicia told her all about Dallas, the store they owned, and how Tony screwed her over. It was obvious that he broke her heart and Marlena figured out quickly that Alicia held onto the hope that she hadn't made a mistake giving up her virginity to Tony. That was something the slimeball held over her head, too, but to know that Alicia's brother was also pressuring her just wasn't right. The poor woman was being controlled and threatened by not only her ex but also her brother. No wonder she was so fearful of entertaining an attraction to Max, Monroe, and Caldwell, but they were real men. These other two were nothing but trouble and they were holding Alicia back from happiness and success, never mind potentially true love.

"I think you need to gain some self-confidence, Alicia. You've allowed your brother and Tony to hold you down for far too long. It doesn't matter that Tony was your first."

"But it makes things worse."

"It shouldn't. Did you love him when you slept with him?"

"Of course."

"Then it shouldn't matter, and obviously he is not the commitment kind. You need to move on and to realize that when you had sex with him and gave up your virginity you loved him. There were real feelings, true emotions, and it wasn't just sex. People grow apart all the time. Throw in how much of a slimeball he turned out to be and you should really have no guilt or regrets. Let that go and move on. He isn't right for you. He's trouble."

"I know that he is. It's not like I have feelings for him still it's just that between him and my brother they have this power over me. It makes me feel guilty and unable to make my own decisions."

"But you left Dallas and you have been surviving on your own and accomplishing things solo without them. You've proven that you don't need either man to survive. You don't need any man to survive and succeed, Alicia, you just need confidence in yourself. You're stronger than you give yourself credit for."

"Then why when they call do I crumble? Why am I practically shaking and feeling like a child caught doing something naughty?"

"Because over the years they manipulated you, controlled you, and forced their demands on you. It's one thing for your lover, your business partner to do those things and hurt you, but it's another for your own brother to assist Tony. I know he's the only family you have, Alicia, but he's holding you down and keeping you from happiness, too."

Alicia began to cry and Marlena felt her own eyes well up with tears. It wasn't fair. Alicia was kind and sweet and she deserved better.

"Everything is going to be okay. You've got me, Adele, and Mercedes. We'd do anything for you just like you would do anything for us. You can't let Tony and Alvin hold you down anymore. You can't let them keep you from the things you want and desire. Like the store and Monroe, Max, and Caldwell."

"Oh God, Marlena. Max, Monroe, and Caldwell can't know about Tony and Alvin. God, they'll think I'm weak and usable."

"No, honey, they would probably react like me and feel angry at what your brother and Tony have been doing. The Gordon men seem like sincerely good men. Real men who put a woman first and who would care for and protect their woman. After all, they live here in Chance and you know how things work. The men protect the women. They stake a claim to be a woman's guardian and then they are truly committed to her. They like you. I'm sure they're waiting for you to let them know you feel the same things for them before they stake that claim. When that happens, Tony and Alvin won't have the opportunity or the ability to hurt you anymore."

"Oh how I wish what you say would come true. But I'm just too unsure, too scared right now to believe there's any man out there that doesn't want to hurt me or use me and control me. The perfect man seems like a fantasy."

"But that's not true. There are three perfect ones waiting until you're ready. Confide in them. Let them in, Alicia, and everything else will fall into place. You'll see."

"I just don't know if I'm capable of taking that chance."

"Oh, I think you're capable, you just need to let go a little and let them inside your heart, and everything else will happen naturally."

Alicia looked unsure.

"Give it a try Monday at their house tomorrow. Continue to talk with them and have normal conversation and feel what's right in front of you. As far as the business is concerned, talk about negotiating an agreement that makes you feel comfortable and still somewhat independent financially. It will all work out. I promise."

Alicia smiled and hugged Marlena. "You're my best friend, Marlena. Thank you."

* * * *

Alicia was getting ready for work as usual. She smiled as she put on the light skirt and tank top along with her tennis sneakers. She added the light green blouse and then turned side to side to see how she looked in the mirror. She smiled then thought about Monroe, Caldwell, and Max. They had been so sweet and conversational all week.

She learned more about them and even talked to their mom on a Skype call as she teased Monroe about his need for a haircut. It was funny, but their mom really seemed to care about them and she was surprised at the envious feeling she had.

Her parents weren't exactly the nicest people. They always struggled with money, fought a lot and complained that they never should have had children. Alicia realized pretty quickly that no matter how much she tried to show them love, her parents didn't reciprocate. Her brother was older, and pushed for all the attention. He wasn't happy either but her parents favored him over her. She never really got over that or how Alvin held it over her head. He would tell her that he would share things with her that their parents only gave him. When her father had an accident at work and was off his feet and their mom was working, Alicia took care of him, but even that didn't gain the man's love. She realized by eighteen that she needed to do things for herself and start making money and saving money. She did that.

She felt the tears in her eyes. Alvin gave her some money here and there. Nothing big, maybe fifty dollars or a twenty, but it was her who went to college, paid for it, worked two jobs and succeeded.

Alvin had it in his head that when their parents died he would get some sort of inheritance. So he didn't work hard or try to make it on his own. When her parents passed away in a car accident all Alvin worried about was this money he thought they had left him. Turned out, any money they had, which was little was used to cover funeral costs and to fix up their small house to sell and get back taxes on.

Alicia remembered thinking that she was finally rid of the sadness, the feelings of inadequacy and not growing up with love and support. She remained close to Alvin despite his negative attitude and he even introduced her to his best friend Tony.

That had been the biggest mistake of her life. Believing Tony's lies, his sincerity and interest in her. He played her like a fiddle and in the end she was broken. Still broken now.

She wiped the tear that rolled down her cheek and looked at herself in the mirror.

Her heart ached, yet longed for the things other women in Chance had. The love, the care and affection of a man or even men. Honest, loyal, true men that would do anything to protect their woman. Alicia wanted to feel safe. She wanted to feel appreciated. She wasn't even sure if anyone could love her or if she lacked what was needed, but at this point she would settle for friendship, companionship and security.

She reached over toward the dresser and sprayed her perfume. It was one that Max liked a lot. In fact, yesterday when he snuck up behind her and sniffed her neck, she thought she might have lost it.

She held her ground despite the obvious sexual chemistry building between them.

She thought about their childhood and stories they shared and learned that their mom Sianne was married to three men. Men that were law enforcement officers and one that was the previous sheriff before his son Max took over. It was honorable and another indication of how perfect they were and how imperfect she was.

She took a deep breath and released it. Her belly tightened and she felt unsure, confused, and maybe even a little down despite how good she always felt around the men. They lifted her spirits, made her laugh, and were terribly good looking. Maybe she was creating this fantasy in her head where they would find her appealing and up to their standards? She wasn't certain, but as the project was now coming to an end, she wasn't sure what would happen next. She wanted to accept their help with opening a storefront. They made her feel capable. Like yesterday when she thought she made a mistake with one of the areas on the stained glass but then it helped her to see the potential in altering the color to bring out a truer brown that was identical to their actual house color. Max had pointed it out, and Monroe even went outside to take a picture of the siding of the house then show her it matched perfectly and told her how brilliant she was. No one ever boosted her confidence like these three men. Maybe she was falling for their actions that were only done out of being respectful courteous men? After all, Sianne did say that the men were a bit wild in their younger days but how she raised them to be respectful and to put a woman first always. She even told Alicia to call her if they acted up. That made her chuckle but Caldwell seemed embarrassed and offended.

She looked at the clock and worried that she might be late. Quickly, she grabbed her things and headed out the door. She loved being around them, but it was her that stated it was all business and nothing more. Now she wished she could let her guard down and maybe take a chance at letting Monroe, Max, and Caldwell into her heart.

* * * *

"Is it Alicia's last day working at your place?" Monroe's mom asked as they talked on the phone. He smiled. The two women had hit it off immediately and once Monroe sent a picture of Alicia's work their mom went crazy with excitement.

"Unfortunately yes it is."

"You sound down. Haven't you told her that you and your brothers like her?"

"Mom, it's more complicated than that. I explained about how we got her to work here."

"Honey, I know that idea of yours backfired somewhat, but you did have the opportunity to get to know her a little more and for her to feel more comfortable with the three of you. Just be honest with her and I'm sure you'll get the response you're hoping for."

"I'll see. She's special. She's different and we don't want to screw this up."

His mom chuckled.

"I can't wait to meet her in person. She looked beautiful through the computer on Skype, and very petite. You three be sure to not overwhelm her, never mind hurt her."

"Mom, really?"

"Monroe, I know how the three of you are and you forget how big you are. Just be gentleman."

Monroe chuckled.

"Okay, Mom, I need to go. Love you."

"Love you, too. Oh, and we'll see you in just a few days. Make sure you invite Alicia over Saturday for dinner and to meet us. I can't wait."

"I'll try, Mom. Thanks."

Monroe disconnected the call and leaned back in the chair. He had a heavy heart. He wanted to be honest with Alicia and let her know how much he and his brothers liked her and wanted to get to know her, but then he would see this look in her eyes, or watch her step back and appear frightened, and it made him wonder more about her past. If someone did hurt her he wanted to prove to her that he and his brothers cared and would protect her. She just seemed resistant to accept that.

He looked at the phone and thought about his brothers. They would be stopping in to see her. Today was going to be her last day working here and they needed to make a move or their chance could be gone forever.

* * * *

Alicia sat outside in the sun by the table and umbrella to have some lunch. She'd brought her own sandwich and drink today. It was beautiful outside and she had been inside all morning working on finishing up the project for the men.

"Hey, I would have made something for you for lunch," Monroe said as he walked out onto the patio joining her.

"Oh that's okay, you've been spoiling me all week," she told him as she absorbed his attire. He was dressed casually today. He wore jeans, a dark blue T-shirt that showed off his bulging muscles, and she could practically smell his cologne before he even made it close to her. She loved the scent. It was light, clean, and appealing.

"I don't mind spoiling you. You're doing a wonderful job and my brothers and I enjoy having you here in our home."

"That's sweet, Monroe."

She took a sip of her ice tea then stared out toward the cabana and pool.

"Do you guys get to go swimming a lot and use that cabana?" she asked.

"Not as often as we would like. Max isn't into parties, and Caldwell and I usually have business parties here a few times a year."

"It looks stunning. Does it have a bathroom and fireplace in it? It looks like that from here."

"When you're finished with lunch I'll show you it. So have you thought about the business deal and the storefront? I spoke with Dwyer and he's willing to make a special deal with us."

She swallowed hard and looked at him. His light blue eyes held hers and he seemed so sincere. Her heart pounded inside of her chest. He was so appealing.

"I have thought about it. I have some concerns."

"Concerns?"

"Yes, and perhaps we could discuss them with Caldwell, too, since he's part of this?"

"That's okay. He'll be by in a little while. Why don't we talk now and maybe I can ease your concerns."

She wiped her mouth with the napkin and then took another sip of ice tea as she packed up her garbage from lunch.

"We can walk and talk if that's more comfortable?" he suggested and she nodded her head.

"Well, I'd love to see the cabana and I do have to get back to work. Okay."

She stood up and Monroe walked with her.

"I was thinking that I don't really want to be financially obligated to you guys for very long. I mean let's say this business takes off but then you decide you want out and I don't have the money to buy out your share. Then what? You sell it all off and I'm left with nothing."

"First of all, that's not how Caldwell and I do business. When we invest in a product, a store, or in this case your talent, we invest with the intention of being in for the long haul. Do things happen and change? Sure but we wouldn't pull out and sell the store leaving you with nothing. That's not good business at all. That's being corrupt, self-centered, and downright sneaky. That's not the kind of businesses Caldwell and I run."

His words touched her in more ways than she could explain. In fact, she needed to turn away and change the subject a moment or she might lose it emotionally. She prayed he wasn't bullshitting, for he said the words she needed to hear.

"This is stunning. My God, I could live out here in this cabana. It's like a small house."

"I love sitting out here sometimes at night with the fire going. It's relaxing," he told her and she stared at him. She absorbed his light brown hair, his sensational body, and how tall he was. He must be about six feet three. He towered over her and especially as she stood there wearing tennis sneakers.

"I bet it's nice."

He looked at her, reached out, and caressed a strand of her hair as he held her gaze.

"You should come over one night and enjoy it with me."

She swallowed hard. *God, he's so appealing.* But that fear of being hurt had her lowering her eyes.

He stepped closer and placed his hand on her waist and one on her shoulder then to her neck and under her hair.

She looked up toward him.

"Are you afraid of me?" he asked her, shocking her.

She opened her mouth to respond and then closed it. How could she respond to him? Yes, he scared her but he also aroused her, made her want to be close to him, but she also felt that for his brothers and she was fighting it to avoid a conflict of interest with personal life and business.

She felt his thumb caress her lower lip and he pressed against her.

"Tell me you're not sacred of me or my brothers. Because if you are then we need to do whatever we can to make you feel safe and secure with us."

"I'm just working for you, Monroe. It's not necessary to make me feel safe and secure when I'll only be here a few days longer."

"No. That's not true. Not when I want you here more than just to work. I want you to join me by a fire at night. I want to get to know you better. I want to…taste you," he said as he stared at her lips. She panicked and pulled away.

"I should get back to work." He grabbed her hand and turned her around. He pulled her close.

"Do you feel it? Are you attracted to me and to my brothers?"

"Monroe, this isn't a good idea."

"Why not?"

"Because we're going to possibly do business together. I don't want there to be a conflict of interest when things don't work out."

"You sound so sure that things couldn't work out on a personal and business level. I'm more optimistic, baby," he said and smiled softly.

"I'm more of a pessimist when it comes to men making promises." She pulled back but he pulled her closer, making her gasp.

This close to him, inhaling his cologne, seeing that intense look in his eyes as she stared way up toward his firm expression did a number on her body.

"Real men don't hurt women and make promises they can't keep. I get the feeling someone hurt you. But I'm not him, nor are my brothers."

He was so serious and intense. She didn't want to face this right now. This was what she was afraid of. She looked way.

"Please, Monroe, don't say such things to me. It will make matters worse."

"How so when we're both feeling this attraction?" he asked.

"It won't work out. Not with having a business relationship."

"You don't know that. Besides, we want to support you, help you in achieving your goals and dreams because that's what good men do for their women."

"But I'm not your woman," she said, her voice cracking.

He smiled softly.

"Oh, we're working on it, but you're resistant. Why?"

She took a deep breath. How could she think with him holding her in his arms and up against his solid, muscular chest? His cologne was invading her senses and making her lose her focus and thought.

"Can you release me? I can't think like this."

"Good, maybe that's a good thing. Maybe you're overthinking this and letting go and just feeling could help you see we're for real?"

She began to shake her head and he cupped her face between his hands and held her gaze.

"Ah hell." He sounded so frustrated and emotional but before she could stop him Monroe kissed her deeply, sending her from a mindful state to a lustful one in no time at all.

She could feel his thigh press between her legs then his hand move down her hip over her ass, pulling her snugger against him. She in return couldn't resist touching him, feeling every inch she could touch with her hands. He devoured her moans, explored her mouth thoroughly with his tongue while he used his hands to explore her body. She felt faint, aroused, ready to burst with pleasure, and it scared her. No one ever made her feel this way from kisses alone.

She tried pulling back but he wouldn't allow it. She felt her body being lifted and then her ass gently hit the granite countertop of the island in the cabana.

He pressed his body between her thighs, causing her skirt to part and his crotch to press snug against her sensitive mound. She wiggled and rocked and he countered against her crotch and she could feel his hard erection. He cupped her breast and she moaned deeper then pulled back.

"Monroe. Oh God, Monroe," she said his name and pressed her palms against his chest as she tried to catch her breath.

He kissed along her throat, her chin, and then her neck. She tilted it upward, loving the feel of his firm, masculine lips against her sensitive flesh. He pulled her thighs around his waist and caressed his palms up her calves and thighs then to her hips until he cupped her breasts with both hands.

"My God you taste and feel incredible."

She felt the tears in her eyes. So instantly she wanted so much more than she could allow. She couldn't let her guard down. She would get hurt again and this time would be worse than before because there were three men who could ruin her completely. It was so crazy to think of Caldwell and Max right now after what she just shared with Monroe, but she did. She felt it and understood that they came as a package. As one.

"Please, Monroe, we have to stop. We shouldn't have done this."

"Why not?"

She heard the voice and swung her head around to see Max standing there in uniform. He looked so hard and commanding as he stepped closer. Monroe didn't stop cupping her breasts or kissing her neck. Her lips parted as she took in the sight of Max as he approached. The uniform, the gun and handcuffs, his entire macho, masculine, sexy appearance had her tilting her face up toward him. He reached out, cupped her cheeks between his hands, and brought his lips down over her mouth.

This was bad. Very, very bad, but felt so good and so right at the same time. He plunged his tongue in deeply and she felt her tank top being pushed up, her bra unclipped in the front and then lips, tongue, and teeth latch onto her nipple and breasts. She moaned and shook as her first orgasm hit her hard, causing Monroe to pull her against him. It felt like he was trying to devour as much as her breast as possible with his mouth.

Max kissed her deeply and ran his hands along her other breast as he tugged on her nipple and feasted on her lips. When he released her lips she panted for breath. "Oh God slow down. Please, I can't take it."

"Yes, you can because you're meant for us."

Caldwell. Oh God, Caldwell was there, too, now. He walked closer and Max stepped to the side only for Caldwell to cup her cheeks and look over her breasts. Her tank top was pushed up nearly to her neck and Monroe was feasting on one of them.

"You look like a goddess, baby. I've dreamt of this, of you allowing us in." He leaned forward and softly kissed her lips. He pulled back and held her gaze as if he were testing the waters, seeing if she were okay with this. It was like he took her words about slowing things down seriously, but she now wanted to taste him, too. She pressed closer and he moved but waited for her to close the distance between their lips. Right before she touched her lips to his, feeling the desire to taste him, Caldwell smirked and she poured all her emotions into that kiss. There was no turning back. She allowed them this close and boy did she want more of them.

* * * *

"I could feast on her for hours," Monroe said and Max mumbled in agreement as he suckled Alicia's breast. Caldwell chuckled as he released her lips and kissed her nose and then her lips again smiling at her. She looked shocked, aroused, and flushed from this intimate moment.

Max and Monroe lifted up and both had a hand on her thigh. She pulled her tank top over her breasts, not bothering with the bra right now.

"Are you okay?" Caldwell asked. She whispered yes but shook her head no. He chuckled.

"I think you'll be just fine," Caldwell told her as he caressed her cheeks with his knuckles. He smiled at her and she looked shocked. Her hazel eyes sparkled.

She slid down off the island, lowering her head. "I should get back to work."

"Oh no, there's a lot for us to discuss," Max said, placing his hand on her waist, stopping her from moving. Caldwell looked at her face go flush and her tank top was so low half her breast was pouring from the top. She was well endowed.

"Like what?" she asked, her voice low and sexy, but seemingly unintentional. She shyly pulled her bottom lip between her teeth.

"Like how this happened," Caldwell said to her as she looked at him.

"Like how it's going to happen again and often," Monroe added. She opened her mouth to speak but then Max spoke.

His hands on his hips and that firm sheriff expression he gave when he meant business. "And how things are going to change around here. We've been patiently waiting for you to realize how we felt."

"What do you mean, Max?" she asked.

He reached out and fixed her tank top. The feel of his thick, hard fingers caressing under the strap and repositioning it aroused her. She shivered with desire.

"We want you, Alicia. Have since the moment we laid eyes on you months ago. We've been patient. Hell, you've pushed us to our limit. God, how we've wanted to touch you, taste you, and claim you ours."

"You have? Why? What is it that you want from me?"

"Everything. All of you. Your heart, your love, whatever you're willing to give," Monroe said to her.

Caldwell watched her hazel eyes fill with tears. She looked away and took an unsteady breath.

"I can't. I'm sorry, but I'm just not capable." She pushed between them and tried running but Caldwell stopped her. He turned her around and held her in his arms as she cried.

"Damn, baby. Talk to us," he said.

"Who hurt you, Alicia? Who made you so untrusting and fearful?" Max asked and Caldwell felt his chest tighten. Was that the case here? Had a man hurt her? He wanted to know everything. He wanted to protect her. He ran his palm along her back and rubbed her there, consoling her as she calmed down.

"We're not him, Alicia. We're not him."

* * * *

Alicia was embarrassed and felt so confused. She loved the way it felt to be with these three men, and she loved how they kissed her and touched her. She wanted more. She wanted the things that bound hearts and souls together when there was truth and honesty, but what if these three men were just out for an affair? A good time and nothing more? Could she accept that? Could she live with herself? She knew the answer was no as the tears stung her eyes. She loved the feel of Caldwell's strong arms holding her. She felt protected. Especially with Max and Monroe there, too. What if they were lying? What if they just wanted sex?

She pulled back.

"I don't sleep around. I won't be part of some game or a list."

"What game? What list?" Max asked.

"A list of women you've had sex with in town and out of town. I won't be another notch in your belt," she said and held Max's gaze.

"Why are you looking at me and saying that? Hell, baby, I haven't been with a woman in over a year's time. I take sex very seriously, too."

"She means the list, Max. You know the one that gossip started about you because no one ever sees you with a woman," Monroe said to him.

"I never heard about a list. Who the hell started that?" Max asked.

"Probably a woman you didn't reciprocate feelings for," Caldwell told him.

Max looked at Alicia. She was so distrusting. What if even this banter back and forth were a game?

She turned around and took a deep breath.

Max caught up with her, wrapped an arm around her waist, and pressed her close. Even his hugs, his embrace felt incredible. She was fighting every sensation.

"Baby, don't believe any of that. I don't sleep around. What I tell you is true. Hell. I'm hard to live with and get along with."

"Ain't that the truth," Monroe said, joining them, acting like he was teasing.

"Don't do that. Don't pretend to banter, to say things like that as if it's true."

"Don't you believe us?" Caldwell asked now standing in front of her.

"I don't know what to believe."

"Believe that we're honest men and that whomever hurt you can't ever do it again when you're ours."

"I care about you, Alicia. I want to get to know you, gain your trust, your love," Max told her then kissed her neck.

"As do we. We're not the bad guys here. You'll need to trust that we're not lying, Alicia," Caldwell told her.

"I think we should sit down and talk about this," Monroe said. She shook her head.

"No. I need to get back to work and I need time to understand this."

"What's to understand? You're attracted to us and we're attracted to you. It's simple," Caldwell told her.

Max released her as she shook her head.

"No, it isn't. This is a different type of relationship. Sex, dating, or whatever is not simple. It's complicated and messy and only leads to sadness and broken hearts. I don't know if I can handle that again, so I need some time," she said.

Monroe took her hand and brought it to his chest.

"Someone hurt you so badly that you think all relationships cause pain? That isn't true, Alicia. Whomever he was he didn't know dick about taking care of a woman and commitment." Her eyes widened and she opened her mouth to speak only to close it.

"I think this is a very bad idea," she said, her voice shaking. Monroe pulled her closer, wrapped his arms around her, and smiled.

"No, baby, it's a great idea. Trust me. I promise this is real and my brothers and I won't ever hurt you." He leaned down and kissed her and before long she was wrapping her arms around his shoulders kissing him back and getting lost in the feel of his arms and the intensity of his kiss. She wanted more, and suddenly getting hurt, losing everything didn't seem as important as feeling these sensations and the desires Monroe, Max, and Caldwell brought out in her.

* * * *

Monroe pulled from Alicia's lips, lifted her up into his arms, and began carrying her over toward the large round lounge chair that could fit them all comfortably. It had an attached awning that hid the sun and a sheer curtain to keep out the bugs and provide privacy. He lay her down and sensed his brothers joining them. Placing his hand on her belly under her tank top, he stared down into her eyes. She lay there looking edible and also very afraid.

"Tell us what exactly you are afraid of and why, and we'll work it out right now," he said to her as he eased his hand under her tank top, teasing her breast but not cupping them.

Yet.

He saw her nipples harden beneath the tank and she squirmed as Caldwell joined her on the other side. Max leaned on his side below and began to caress her calf.

She looked at them then back to him.

"It's not that easy," she told him.

"Sure it is," he said, easing higher and letting his fingers graze the underside of her breasts.

"Monroe," she whispered. He kissed her neck.

"Yes, baby."

Caldwell pressed his palm over her belly and hip then up under her tank top. "You have some body on you, Alicia. A body I can't wait to explore."

She pressed her hand over Caldwell's.

"We need to slow down. This isn't fair. The three of you against one."

"Awe, baby, I can guarantee that three on one will be quite the exciting experience for you," Caldwell said then cupped her breast and ran his thumb back and forth over her nipple. Monroe chuckled but Alicia pushed his hand down and sat up. She crossed her arms over her chest.

"That's what I mean. You guys are seducers. That's not what I need in my life."

She went to move and Monroe placed his hand on her belly while Max stood up and crossed his arms in front of his chest.

"Now wait one minute. We are not seducers. Sure we're experienced and a bit older than you are but we're mature enough to know what we want, and we want you, Alicia. In fact, if you're willing to give us an ounce of trust we'll prove to you that we're honest, caring men. Hell, we can be demanding, but guaranteed you'll love it," he told her and Monroe heard her gulp.

"You're very sure of yourself, Sheriff Gordon."

He raised one eyebrow up at her comment.

"And you're skating on thin ice calling me sheriff."

"Well, you are the sheriff. You probably have an image to keep. One that keeps people guessing what you're up to. With all the attention you get from the ladies, I don't know if I want to be part of the local gossip."

He uncrossed his arms. "People talk, Alicia. Ain't nothing I can do about that. Nothing anyone says or thinks matters to me, but my brothers, and you do, and I'll protect what's mine with all I've got. You take your time to think that over, and when you realize I'm the real thing, that I will protect you with all I have to offer, then we'll talk, just you and I."

Monroe was shocked by his brother's tone and words but they seemed to affect Alicia as she pulled her bottom lip between her teeth and nodded her head.

"I need to head back to work. You two take your time with her and let her know that we're not going anywhere," he said and winked at her before he headed out of the cabana and into the house to leave.

Monroe clutched her chin and stared down into her eyes.

"Tell us about your bad experience, Alicia, and we'll tell you anything you want to know about us."

She stared at him and then looked at Caldwell.

"It's not that easy, Monroe."

He ran his palm along her belly and held her gaze. She was so sweet, petite, and beautiful. It was hard to not want to explore her body further and bring her pleasure, but it seemed she was legitimately on guard and he wanted to know why.

"Let's try this. Why don't you ask us some questions? What would you like to know?" Caldwell asked, drawing her attention to him.

She pulled her bottom lip between her teeth and so badly Monroe wanted to coax it out with his own lips and kiss her breathless. He wanted her pliant, accessible, and in his arms.

"I don't know what to ask."

"Just think of something. Anything you want to know."

"How many women have you brought here?" she asked and Monroe was shocked.

"Not one. Our home is private. It's our retreat from work and from business. Usually, that is," Caldwell said then caressed her belly.

Alicia shivered like his touch gave her the goose bumps.

She seemed skeptical.

"Don't believe him?" Monroe asked her and held her gaze.

"I don't know you well enough to tell if you're lying or telling the truth."

"Well, we don't lie. Maybe tell a fib here and there, but for the most part we're honest men. We're being honest with you," Caldwell said.

"I'm sorry. I'm not good at this."

"Good at what? Asking two men some personal questions?" Caldwell pushed.

"I'm not good at talking with any men." She lowered her eyes and Monroe couldn't help but be aroused by her sweetness and natural submissive tendencies. She hadn't a clue what these little signs did to his body, to his dominant side, but he read people well and Alicia needed guidance and a bit of persuasion.

He trailed a finger along her waist then over her breast and nipple.

"We're easy men to talk to. After all, we shared a passionate kiss and I did taste these luscious breasts of yours."

Her lips parted and her cheeks turned a nice shade of pink.

"That's what I mean, Monroe." She sat up and reached under her tank top to reclip her bra. He leaned on his elbow and watched her try to maneuver the large mounds back into confinement as she struggled.

"Don't let him get under your skin. He's harmless and likes to tease. After all, you look pretty sexy when you're flustered and turned on," Caldwell informed hr.

"What makes you think that I'm flustered and turned on?" she asked, voice cracking.

"Just a guess," Caldwell teased her now and she gave him an annoyed expression.

"So you don't play games huh, Caldwell?" she challenged. Caldwell leaned closer and ran his finger along her jaw as he held her gaze.

"Oh, I didn't say I don't play games. In fact, games can be quite fun with the right partner if she's willing."

Monroe chuckled. He couldn't help himself. Alicia looked shocked and aroused.

"Whose doing the teasing now, Caldwell?"

"I can't resist. She asked for it." Caldwell leaned forward and kissed Alicia. That kiss grew deeper and soon Caldwell was moving between her thighs and cupping her cheeks.

"You're a petite little thing. I'm not crushing you, am I?" he asked once he released her lips. She was breathing heavily as she shook her head. Caldwell glanced down at her abundant breasts pouring from the tank that stretched from the way he covered her.

"Good. Because I feel very protective of what's mine, and my brothers'. Very protective." He trailed kisses along her jaw, her lips, and she eased upward to receive more when he pulled back. Caldwell moved slightly to the side and cupped her breast.

"She has a body and a mouth made for us, Monroe. Max is going to love this mouth."

"My mouth?" she asked, seemingly confused. This time Monroe chuckled as he joined his brother touching Alicia and caressing her skin. He teased along her lips and tilted her face toward him.

"Another time we'll explain. But for now, we want you to feel comfortable with us. If we say or do something that frightens you or confuses you, don't hesitate to ask us to stop or to explain. We're willing to take our time with you, Alicia, because our feelings and this attraction are strong. Can you admit to feeling it, too?" Monroe asked her.

She was silent and she moved only her eyes to look from him to Caldwell.

"You feel it, too, don't you, Alicia?" Caldwell asked.

"I do," she whispered, and it seemed to Monroe that saying those words and admitting to feeling the attraction hurt for her to say it.

"You're not heading to a death sentence, Alicia. This is a good thing, you'll see."

"I don't know. I'm not really the relationship type and I have so much going on right now. Besides, you two want to partner up and work a business deal with me. Things will go wrong. You'll hate me."

"No. That's not going to happen. We'll put in any safeguards you want and feel comfortable with," Monroe told her.

"Alicia, maybe if you explain about your bad business experience it may help us understand your concerns. Can you share it with us?" Caldwell asked, sitting up. Monroe did the same as Alicia sat up, too, and crossed her legs.

She looked away from them and took a few breaths. Monroe could see that Caldwell was becoming impatient. Thank goodness Max weren't here or he would demand answers. His brother had the least patience of the three of them.

"I had a boyfriend and we went into business together. I had saved a lot of money and fronted most of the cost for the small store. It was in a great location on a tourist strip in Dallas. We sold lots of cool items from local artists and we were doing great. He had some ideas that were different from mine. I knew a successful business required a hands-on approach to ensure things got done and the store was successful. He enjoyed spending money we made and well, cheating on me."

"What?" Caldwell asked and Monroe was at a loss for words.

She scooted down off the lounge chair and stood up fixing herself.

"Well, long story short, he sold the business out from under me. So he screwed me over, broke my heart, left me broke and financially unstable, and blamed it all on me. I never saw a penny of the payoff which supposedly was a loss but that was bullshit. I trusted him with more than I've ever trusted anyone in my life. So you see, it's not a good idea that you guys want to do business together."

Monroe stood up and placed his hands on her shoulders.

"Baby, we're not like your ex-boyfriend. That guy sounds like a total asshole. No offense." She chuckled and turned away.

"I'm sorry, but this isn't going to work out any way we look at it. I'll finish up the job today with the stained glass in the winery, but I think it's best if we remain friends."

"Not happening, Alicia," Caldwell said and walked around the lounge chair and took her hand, pulling her close.

"Alicia, it's time to move on and put the past behind you. Give us a chance to show you how real men treat their women. We'll work out the details of the business deal. We could hold a loan and act as a bank for you and you can make payments to us, no interest."

Her eyes widened and Monroe had to hide his smile. Never in a million years would Caldwell make such an offer. He would charge interest. That was what kept them making money.

"You would do that for me?" she asked, her voice soft and timid. Monroe placed his hands on her shoulders from behind and now she was sandwiched between them.

"That's an offer I've never given anyone. But for you, I'd do it if that would show you how trustworthy my brothers and I are."

"So what do you say?" Monroe asked her.

"I should think about it."

"No, you should jump on the offer because it's only on the table right now."

She smiled. "Then yes, I accept."

"Wonderful. Now let's seal it with a kiss," Caldwell told her.

She ran her hands up his chest to his shoulders to stand on her tiptoes, but he still had to lower slightly. "Is that legal Caldwell?" she teased.

"It is when it's your lips pressed against mine, Alicia."

Caldwell kissed her and Monroe smiled wide. This was going to work out just fine.

"This is going to be the beginning of a very special partnership," Monroe said and after Caldwell released Alicia's lips, Monroe kissed her next.

Chapter 5

Max leaned back against the table, arms crossed, eyes glued to Alicia's hips and the way her flair skirt tapped against her thighs. She had to come back this morning to finish up the stained glass piece. Monroe and Caldwell were due here momentarily, but had informed him of their conversation with Alicia once he left for work yesterday. His cock hardened beneath his uniform pants as he thought about her submissive personality and how protective he felt over her.

"That should do it," she said. Her sweet, calm voice had a way of soothing over the tense feelings he had trying to hold back and take things slow.

He wanted to pull her into his arms, or bend her gently over the wine-tasting table and explore under her skirt.

She glanced at him and her expression changed. She looked concerned, aroused…sexy.

She swallowed hard and lowered her eyes.

"Alicia," he said her name, not realizing until the words left his lips how demanding, firm, and deep his tone was. She jerked her head upward.

He didn't uncross his arms.

"Come here."

He absorbed the way she worried her bottom lip and slowly walked closer. He intimidated her and even that turned him on.

The moment she was within reach, and once his eyes explored her sexy figure and abundant breasts peeking out from the sleeveless cream blouse she wore, he couldn't resist.

He snagged her around the waist, pulled her close, and kissed her deeply.

When he felt her palms against his chest rubbing up and down his pectoral muscles and making his cock throb for release he wanted to exhale in relief, but he was too turned on, too aroused and needy for a bit more of Alicia. He ran his hands under her skirt and against her bare thigh, bringing it higher against his thigh.

She moaned into his mouth and he deepened the kiss as he used his palm to explore the crack of her ass. He slid fingers underneath the thin material of what had to be thong panties and maneuvered a finger to her cunt.

"Oh," she gasped, pulling her mouth from his only for him to press deeper and stroke upward. His grip around her waist was snug and his expression heated and intense as he held her shocked gaze.

"You're wet and hot, Alicia. That's real sexy."

"Oh God, Max, please. Oh." She moaned and tilted her head back.

He licked her neck, nibbled on a sensitive spot that had her pussy leaking cream.

"Fuck, baby, I need more of you."

He pulled back, pulled fingers from her cunt, and maneuvered her to his liking.

He wrapped his arms around her waist and kissed the corner of her mouth as he spoke softly to her. He was on fire. He was so damn needy to taste her.

"This wine-tasting table is no longer just for tasting wine."

He lifted her up by her hips and slowly lowered her back to the table, being careful that she didn't bang her head on the hard wood. He kissed her lips and ran his hands up her thighs, spreading them as he pushed his body between them.

Alicia moaned and ran her fingers through his hair.

"I want to taste you. You'll let me," he asked but it came out as a demand and he held his breath, waiting to see if he fucked up and scared her. She nodded her head, shocking him as she ran her delicate fingers through his hair.

He couldn't help but smile as he eased back, taking the thin material of her panties downward and then dropping them to the floor.

He pressed her skirt upward and his eyes locked onto her glistening cunt.

"You wet for me, Alicia?" he asked her and her cheeks turned a nice shade of pink. He lowered his mouth closer as he chuckled and she squirmed from his warm breath colliding against her pussy lips.

"Please, Max, don't tease me. God, I can't believe I'm doing this."

He stroked a finger along her pussy lips then held her gaze.

"I'm a demanding man, Alicia. There's things I want and expect from you. The longer I wait to claim this body the more intense my needs become."

She parted her lips and breathed a little heavier.

He stroked just the tip of his thumb up into her pussy.

"Max," she said and gripped his wrist.

He shook his head and made a noise. "Tsk, tsk. Release my wrist. Raise your hands above your head and offer me this pussy to taste." He pressed his thumb a little deeper but not all the way.

"Oh God you're wild. This is insane."

"What's insane is these feelings I have for you, Alicia. This burning, aching need to claim every inch of you. To fuck this pussy as you cry out my name and then fuck this ass." He stroked his thumb downward, letting her pussy cream coat her anus. He felt the muscle tighten up as she gasped.

"Oh God, Max." She slowly rocked her hips.

"Ever get fucked in the ass, Alicia?" She shook her head so quickly he had to chuckle.

"Well it's going to feel real good when I'm fucking this pussy while Monroe fucks this ass and Caldwell strokes his cock into that sweet sexy mouth of yours," he told her as he used his other finger to trail across her lips then press into her mouth.

The little minx licked his finger and suckled it. His eyes widened and his heart raced.

"You sassing me, girl?" he asked. Then he pulled his finger from her mouth and trailed it down her throat over her breasts, pinching her nipple as he moved his thumb and replaced it with two fingers, stroking her pussy. He thrust his fingers in and out of her cunt as she wiggled, moaned, and panted.

"That's it, baby. Don't you come now. You wait until I get my fill." He lowered down and pushed her blouse and camisole aside to lick her breasts and pull on the bud as his fingers thrust faster.

"Max, oh God, Max, please. I can't take it."

"You will take it."

He lowered down and pulled his fingers from her pussy and replaced them with his mouth. He suckled her pussy lips, tugged on her clit, and feasted on her cream as she flowed like a faucet. He cupped her breasts and she thrust her pussy downward. He was aroused and wild knowing that she kept her hands above her head as he instructed and hadn't moved.

She grunted and moaned.

He pulled his mouth from her cunt.

"That's my girl. You keep those hands up and you obey my orders."

"Oh God, Max. Please, please, please, let me come," she cried out and he could see the tears in her eyes as she moaned and thrashed side to side.

"Come for me now," he said then latched onto her pussy with his mouth and suckled hard.

Her screams filled the room and echoed around the walls. She thrashed and moaned as he suckled and feasted on her delicious cream until her moans softened and her legs fell over his shoulders limp.

"What in God's name?" He heard the fast footsteps and knew her screams had alarmed his brothers. Max caressed her thighs and held her gaze. Monroe and Caldwell emerged from the staircase, concerned expressions on their faces that instantly turned to pleasure.

"What do we have here?" Monroe asked, moving closer.

"Alicia thought there was a better use for this wine-tasting table than wine," Max whispered as he stroked her thighs and smirked at her.

"What else could it be used for?" Caldwell asked, caressing her arms that remained above her head.

"Tasting pussy," Max whispered and he saw her eyes darken and her thighs tightened up again.

"I think that's a really great idea. In fact, I could use a little taste myself," Monroe said and then leaned down and kissed Alicia on the lips.

Max lowered her thighs and Caldwell took his position between her legs.

When Monroe released her lips, Caldwell stroked a finger up into her cunt.

She gasped and Monroe cupped her breast.

"Look at you. All spread out on our tasting table, the rays of the sun cascading through the stained glass portrait you made. You look like a goddess, Alicia. You're so beautiful."

"And obedient," Max added as he caressed her arms that remained above her head. He leaned down and kissed between her one elbow and upper arm where it bent.

"Do you like handing over all control to me? Do you like how it makes you feel?" he asked her then traced a finger along her lips.

"Yes."

"Why is that? What did you feel as I stroked and feasted on this sweet pussy and ordered you to keep your hands above your head, to not come until I said so? What did you feel?"

"Free. Alive, Max," she said and a tear escaped from her eye.

He leaned down and wiped it away then cupped her cheek.

She moaned as Caldwell stroked a finger deeper into her cunt.

"That's what being our woman, our lover will be like. Freedom, being cared for and adored."

"Being put first in everything we do," Monroe added and smiled softly.

"Give us all of you, Alicia, and we promise to take care of you, protect you, and make you feel this good, this loved and cherished for the rest of your life," Max whispered as he held her jaw while Monroe stroked her cunt and Monroe traced tiny circles over her nipple above the camisole.

"Oh God yes. Yes, I want that. I want to believe you."

"But?"

"I'm scared. I've only had one lover. Ever. The three of you are so, so big, sexy, intimidating, and perfect. I'm." She lowered her eyes.

"Perfect, too," Monroe and Max said at the same time.

"We'll show you. Let us in, Alicia. Let us take you together. Make love to you together and you'll see how perfect this will be," Caldwell whispered.

Max felt his heart racing. He wanted her so badly his cock throbbed and his heart ached with desire.

"I must be out of my mind. Yes. Yes, I want you, too. I want to trust you, to believe you. Please make me feel alive, free, like a desirable woman, not one scorned and brokenhearted, fearful, and weak. Please. Please be real."

"Oh we're real, and you, beautiful, are going to be our woman officially and in every way," Caldwell told her as he eased a finger from her pussy and lifted her up into his arms.

She wrapped her legs around his waist.

"To the bedroom. We're going to make Alicia all ours and explore every inch of this sexy body and make her scream for more," Max said then cupped her cheek and kissed her deeply before they headed upstairs to make love to Alicia for the very first time.

* * * *

Alicia's heart was pounding inside of her chest. Was she making a huge mistake? She didn't know and after the way they aroused her body, making her needy for more, she knew she had to do this. This was the first huge decision she'd made since the Dallas bullshit. She thought about Tony. Not because she felt guilty or as if she were about to cheat on him, but she couldn't help but compare these men to him. Hands down, the Gordon men dominated in every area. Max? Oh God Max made her feel things no one else ever bought out in her. Who would have known she was so submissive and wanted to be dominated in the bedroom?

She reached up and touched Caldwell's chin then kissed the tip of it. His hold on her tightened as if her simple touch was too much for him to handle. It made her feel some control, but she preferred letting them lead.

"Are you okay?" Caldwell asked her as he lowered her feet to the bedroom rug.

"I'm scared, Caldwell. Scared that I could be making a huge mistake, yet not knowing, not feeling more of what you, Monroe, and Max bring out in me, scares me more."

He caressed her cheek and rested his wrist against her neck as he smiled softly, sincerely at her.

"This is not a mistake. In our lives, in our bed with our cocks deep inside of you is where you belong. No one can hurt you. No one will criticize you, question your judgment, and make you feel inadequate, obsolete, or meaningless here. On the contrary, my sweet, sensual Alicia, this is where you're free. Where we want you to let go and just breathe."

The tears stung her eyes. The meaning of his words hit closer to home than she believed Caldwell knew. But somehow he nailed it. Somehow these three men touched her in a place no one had ever gotten to or that she knew existed. It was like she waited for them all her life, and now they were here.

She felt the second set of hand on her shoulder, then lips press against her skin.

She relished in the moment, knowing that Monroe was touching her, too. She looked for Max but couldn't see him.

"Max is here. He's getting things ready. We want you comfortable, and more than ready for the three of us," Monroe said then tilted her face toward him to the side and kissed her deeply.

They undressed her slowly, letting their masculine hands caress, massage, arouse her body inch by inch. She felt every sensation so deeply. The pressure of a masculine hand against her hip bone, a caress to her ass cheek, a stroke of a finger along her pussy lips. It was everything she ever longed to feel, and at the same time frightening to be letting go so easily. Was she being easy? How could that be when she'd waited forever to feel like this and be touched like this. She prayed it was as meaningful for them as it was for her.

She was naked and it didn't faze her except to make her mind wonder if they liked what they saw. She wanted to be sexy for them, soft for them, ready for whatever they wanted to take from her and give to her. She looked them over with hunger in her core and certainly it showed in her body as her nipples hardened from their stares and slow, teasing strokes of their fingers.

Her lips parted but she absorbed all she could about them and this moment. Monroe and Caldwell were only in their dress pants, belts undone, and looking sexy as ever. Caldwell had light brown hair on his head but a small patch of darker hair in almost an uneven line that led from under his belly button down his underwear. She licked her lips and looked at Monroe. He was bare, smooth, and showing no hair anywhere. She imagined licking his skin, tasting his nipples, and trailing her tongue along every ridge of muscle and taking her time to enjoy both their bodies.

Monroe stroked her nipple as Caldwell stroked her cunt, teasing the outer layers and making her moan and cream while she slowly rocked her hips. She wanted to feel his digit inside of her, his cock buried deep as she let go and allowed them to do as they pleased with her. She wanted to feel alive, real, an attractive, desirable woman. She felt the emotion run rampant through her bloodstream. Her eyes welled up with tears and Monroe kissed her and brought her pleasure. Then just as quickly he released her lips and kissed her again. He repeated the motion, holding her gaze each time he pulled back. The connection was so intense she looked away only for him to reprimand her. "Look at me. Don't turn away. Don't fear what we have between us."

He cupped her cheeks and kissed her deeply again, exploring her mouth with his tongue and with vigor. Caldwell cupped her breasts then kissed her belly as he knelt on the floor in front of her.

Caldwell pulled back.

"Undress us. Explore what's yours, Alicia."

She shivered from the thought. They were hers. They were her men, and their bodies belonged to only her right now.

She reached out and stroked Caldwell's jaw.

"You're so handsome. You and your brothers are gorgeous," she told him and he shook his head and gripped her hips.

"You're the gorgeous one, Alicia."

She smiled then reached out and undid his pants and pushed them down. She gasped at the size and girth of his cock. It was long, thick, and dripped with pre-cum. She licked her lips.

"Taste me if you want to. If you're comfortable," he said.

She took a deep breath and could already get a scent of him. She lowered down, cupped his balls, and then his cock.

"Sweet mercy," he said, eyes closed and shoulders back. She stroked his cock and he slowly moved his hips.

"Legs apart," Monroe ordered her as he pressed up against her back, kneeling on the floor behind her.

She did as he said.

"That's a good girl. You'll be rewarded," Max said, interrupting and adding in. She shivered and tightened up knowing Max was there, too, and watching her. It made her feel intimidated and uncertain. He was so damn authoritative and she wanted to please him and hear him tell her how good she was and holy crap, obedient to his wishes.

She felt Monroe's hands widen her thighs, then his palm moved down her back, making her lower forward. She wasn't sure what he wanted but then she saw Caldwell's cock and she knew what to do. She opened her mouth and licked the tip. Caldwell moaned and she slid her mouth lower until she could take his cock deeper and she gagged. She pulled back then readjusted. Then she felt the fingers to her cunt from behind and Monroe pressing over her as he thrust fingers into her pussy.

"Are you on the pill?" Max asked and she nodded her head as she continued to suck on Caldwell's cock. He ran his fingers through her hair and pumped his hips slowly. Behind her Monroe thrust fingers into her pussy and then pulled back.

"Your skin is perfect. So silky and soft. I don't see any tan lines. How exactly is that?" he asked.

Smack.

She jerked not expecting the spank to her ass.

She looked at Max as he lowered closer to her.

"You sunbathing in the nude?" he asked with an intense expression and she felt her cheeks warm and tried to focus on Caldwell's cock but Max was so intense.

"Where?" he asked.

Caldwell pulled from her mouth.

"Answer him. Where are you lying out naked in the sun?"

She was panting and entirely too turned on by this.

"On my back porch."

"At your home where you don't lock the doors?" Max asked.

She nodded.

Smack.

"Monroe," she gasped, not expecting him to smack her ass next and then felt his fingers move from her pussy to her anus. They pushed in slowly and she gasped.

"Anyone can see you up there. No more. Only here at our place with one of us watching over you. Got it," Max stated.

She nodded her head. He smiled as he ran his palm along her ass and hip.

"You're our woman. No one else gets to see this sexy body and fuck this sexy body but the three of us."

He cupped her cheek and kissed her deeply as Monroe continued to arouse her anus. She was rocking her hips, moaning and shaking, feeling her pussy swell with need to be touched. Max released her lips.

"Oh, Max, please. Please do something," she begged. Actually begged for it.

"She's made for us, Max. She's ours," Monroe said and pulled his finger from her anus. As she took a deep breath, Max lifted her up off her knees as if she weighed nothing at all and held her in his arms.

"Do you want us?" he asked her.

"Yes."

He smiled softly.

"We're going to take you together. We want you to experience making love to the three of us together as what this relationship is going to be for now on. No comparisons to others, because nothing from the past compares."

Oh God how can he know me so well and know what I'm thinking. Am I going to hell for this? For wanting three men? For having three men at once?

He lay back on the bed, muscles galore staring back at her, holding her gaze and adjusting her body. Strong, hard thigh muscles pressed up against hers as she straddled him and instantly felt his thick, hard cock. She could hardly breathe. Would it fit? She didn't think so.

"Easy, baby. Let Caldwell and Monroe get that ass ready for cock, while I get this pussy ready."

He shifted her upward and she had to grab onto his shoulders to stop from falling on him. Then as his mouth found her clit she realized that was exactly what Max wanted. Her pussy over his face so he could feast on her, literally.

Someone pressed her back lower but she didn't focus on that. She focused on the feel of Max's tongue and finger coaxing out her cream and making her pussy vibrate and leak. The pressure of his thick, hard fingers penetrating her ass cheeks and hip bone as he feasted on her pussy and cream. She moved her hips and he sucked her clit harder and harder, making it feel swollen and needy. She ran her fingers through his hair and then gripped the comforter to maintain some balance above him.

She felt a tongue kissing and licking her ass cheeks then a second one kissing and licking the other ass cheek and she relaxed and enjoyed it. When a tongue licked along her anus she gasped and tightened.

"Relax," Monroe said and squeezed her ass.

She tried until she felt the cool liquid against her anus then fingers pressing into her ass. It burned, it aroused her, and she began to moan as all three men set out to get her ready for them.

When Monroe knelt on the bed holding his cock she didn't think twice. She reached for it and stroked it up and down.

Max pulled his mouth from her cunt and Caldwell fingered her ass. It was all too much as she moaned and shook.

"Damn, baby," Max said and quickly licked her pussy, slurped and suckled her clit, making her feel weak and ready for anything.

He pulled back.

"Delicious. She's ready for us."

He slid her hips downward.

"Take my cock inside of you, Alicia. Make me yours. Then suck on Caldwell's cock and get ready to relax and let Monroe fuck that sexy ass."

She could hardly breathe his words turned her on so much. His directions, his orders, how easily he talked about putting a cock in every hole. She imagined it as she felt her body respond and cream some more.

She eased back, trying not to lose it with every stroke of a finger into her ass. Monroe was thrusting his digit faster, deeper as she reached for Max's cock and aligned it with her pussy before sinking down. She gasped and shuddered. They were so big.

"You can take us. We're meant for you and this body. Show us. You're in control right now. Only what you want matters."

"No, Max, what we all want matters. I want you to want from me, too."

Max reached up and caressed her neck under her hair.

"Sweet Alicia, we do want from you. We want everything, but we know this is a first and that you may need time to adjust. Take it. Take whatever you want. We're not going anywhere."

She eased his cock up into her pussy and lowered deeply.

As she moved up and down the deep, full sensation intensified as she moaned and rocked her hips slowly.

"That's it. Just like that," Monroe told her. She looked at Caldwell and locked gazes with him.

He stroked his cock and tempted her with those sexy eyes of his.

Feeling exceptional, she lowered her mouth to his cock and slowly took him into her mouth. This alone with Max thrusting his cock up into her pussy felt so naughty, but as she got the hang of thrusting and sucking, she felt Monroe pull his fingers from her ass and kiss each mound. She wanted to demand he go back in and touch her, but then she felt the cool liquid again and the tip of Monroe's cock. She was about to have anal sex, and surprisingly she wanted it, craved it badly.

"Relax and enjoy it. Don't resist," Max said and Monroe eased his cock into her ass while Caldwell thrust slowly into her mouth and Max thrust slowly upward. He held himself steady and when Monroe was fully in her ass they all moaned.

"Holy mother, she's so fucking tight," Monroe said and began to thrust into her ass.

She felt her body tighten up and knew she would come.

She grunted and Caldwell moaned as he came. She drank from his cock, licked and cleaned it until he fell backward off the bed.

Max moved up and down, thrusting his hips, penetrating her cunt as Monroe stroked his cock into her ass and smacked each cheek.

She cried out her first orgasm and then Monroe came in her ass. He calmed his breathing and pulled out, and that was when Max took over. He rolled her to her back, lifted her thighs higher with his cock still embedded in her cunt, and he began a series of slow, deep thrusts. Her pussy ached with need. Her breath caught in her throat. He grabbed her hands, placed them above her head, their fingers entwined, and he rammed his cock faster.

"Yes, Max. Yes, harder, more," she begged and he gave her more than she could handle as the bed rocked. She screamed out his name and came just as he followed, too.

Max rolled her to the side and began kissing her as he eased his cock out of her sensitive pussy. "You're ours now, Alicia. You're fucking incredible and we'll never get enough of you. Ever." He told her how much he cared about her and how perfect this was going to be.

She sure hoped so, because if things worked out and she became the lover of three men, when her brother found out, he may try to get her admitted into a mental institution. He would do anything to get her money, her help financially so he wouldn't have to raise a finger. She suddenly felt protective of Monroe, Caldwell, and Max. No one would come between them. No one.

Chapter 6

"Alvin, have you spoken to your sister?" Tony asked as he sat at the table in the crowded restaurant and watched some sexy brunette walk by. He checked out her ass and smiled. He caught her eye and gave a wink. Her smile as she made her way to the bar a few feet away was encouraging.

"No. I haven't spoken to her in over a week. I called but she doesn't call back."

He became angry.

"I told her that she needed to call you back whenever you tried and she missed the call. What could possibly be going on?"

"Maybe her eBay business and the stained glass art she makes is taking off. Who the hell knows. I haven't seen a check from her in quite some time. How is that settlement going from the old business you guys shared and sold out? You should be getting money by now."

Tony smiled to himself. Alvin and his sister would never see a cent of that money. It was his, just like Alicia would be his again. He thought about her a lot. How innocent she was. How he took her virginity. Being with all these women lately and fucking them every which way was making him crave Alicia. She needed him. He could manipulate her with only a few words. Power like that over a woman didn't come along often. Plus if she were making some money and possibly getting famous, her art could be raking in the dough big time.

"If it is then she'll need my help. You know your sister doesn't know shit about running a business and marketing herself. That's why I had to save our asses and sell out the business in Dallas. I don't want to see that coming her way. I know we're not an item anymore, but considering how close we were and how we almost got married, I feel kind of obligated to protect her."

"I appreciate that, Tony. She doesn't though. Maybe you shouldn't bother."

"Are you kidding me? You'll have money coming to you, too. For all the aggravation. Do you have an address for her in that town in South Carolina?"

"Yeah, it's called Chance. I can send you the exact address in a little while. I have to find it. But I know she's living above a garage or something. She said it was nice."

"She needs me, Alvin. She's probably living in shit."

"It's kind of you to still care after what she did and how she left you. Do you think there's a possibility you two can make amends and maybe get married?"

"It's what I'm hoping for. You know Alicia, she aims to please and is a very hard worker. I'll expect her to sing a different tune when I get together with her. No more taking it easy on her. She needs to learn that a man is in charge and a good woman is there to support him and encourage him. She may need some hard discipline."

"Maybe you ought to wait until you see her to decide if you still want her. Life alone can harden a woman and make her ugly. She may have even gained weight or stopped caring about her looks."

Tony shivered at the thought. Alicia was well endowed and had a body like a centerfold model. No way would she let herself go. Even struggling to make ends meet she kept herself tidy and looking pretty. It would be fun to have to train her and make her into the woman he needed and desired. What pissed him off was that he would have to be patient. She was shy, only had him as a lover, and his sexual appetite was different then. He wanted every part of her, and every part of her he would have.

"I'll let you know if and when I decide to go see her. I want to look deeper into this town first. It might be wiser to have her leave there and take her elsewhere. Who knows who is sniffing around her and trying to gain her trust."

"I thought about that, too. She's naive and vulnerable. I hope she's okay."

"She will be once I have her. Don't worry. Let me take care of everything."

"And what about the money?" Alvin asked.

"You'll be the first to know when I get it and if I get it. There's always some sort of scam. I hope we all didn't get screwed by that woman and her husband who bought us out. Who knows. Talk to you soon, Alvin."

He hung up the phone and glanced at the bar. The brunette was sitting there glancing at him. Legs crossed, girly tropical drink in her hand, and he nodded for her to come over. She smiled, grabbed her purse and drink, and made her way over, hips moving, looking ready for action.

Oh yeah, he was going to get some today and tomorrow he would make the plans to find his Alicia and make her beg forgiveness and to be his once again.

* * * *

Alicia trailed her fingers, along Max's muscles on his chest as she lay in bed by his side. Behind her Monroe traced the curves of her hips and then lower toward her pussy. When his lips touched the skin on her shoulder she closed her eyes and exhaled.

"What are you thinking about right now?" Monroe asked her.

"I know what I'm thinking about right now," Caldwell said as he picked up the tube of lube and tapped it against his palm.

"None of that right now. This was a first for her and she needs to recover," Max said firmly, and Caldwell chuckled as he dropped the tube on the bed then cuddled up by her calves and feet. Max lifted her chin to look at her.

"Are you sore?"

She shook her head.

"Don't lie to me. I'll know it immediately," he told her and she knew he would. He was a sheriff, plus he seemed to have an ability to tell a lot about a person. She didn't want to admit to being sore but she was. She'd never had sex like she just did and never with three men. Everything felt different. Her pussy felt needy even now, after making love to Max. Her mouth felt achy from sucking on Caldwell's cock which she had never liked doing to Tony but only did it a handful of times. She shifted a little and sure enough her ass hurt slightly. More like a burn, but as she thought about how Monroe took her there, how he eased the lube in her ass, fingered her to stretch her muscles to be sure she could handle his cock, she felt aroused all over again. Could this type of relationship be the one for her? The one she longed for forever?

"Hey, talk to us. What are you feeling? Be honest now," Max coaxed her then looked at her lips, pressed a gentle kiss to them, and pulled back holding her gaze.

"Needy," she whispered in a husky voice.

Caldwell jumped up.

"Told you."

"Slow down. We don't want to hurt you or make you feel any pain," Max said and then rolled her to her back. He played with her nipple then cupped her breast. When he leaned lower and nibbled a sensitive spot on her neck, she reached up to touch him, run her fingers through his hair, and find his mouth with hers.

She kissed his chin, nibbling on the light gruff along there and to his firm lips.

He opened for her and she delved her tongue deeply, exploring his mouth.

She loved how he tasted, how it felt to caress his skin, feel the dusting of hair along his chest and to know he was hers to explore. She eased her leg over his waist and straddled him, kissing him, rocking her hips against him until she felt the fingers stroke her pussy from behind.

Max lifted her up under her arms and took back control of the situation. He held her gaze.

"I want you to ride, Monroe. He needs to feel how tight and needy this cunt of yours is, baby. I want you to ride him good."

It was wild, but Max had a voice, a way about him that aroused her senses and made her want to please him and obey him. Her heart soared in adoration and as she looked into Monroe's light blue eyes, she realized she felt the same way about him.

"Scoot down lower, Monroe. I have some exploring of my own to do," Caldwell said and she felt his hands on her hips and Monroe eased to the edge of the bed.

They arranged her to their liking. Max disappeared a moment and she lowered to kiss Monroe.

His hands felt so good as they caressed her arms, her back, and then her ass. When he ran a finger down the crack of her ass, she moaned into his mouth.

Then she felt Caldwell's hands widening her ass cheeks. Monroe pulled his hands away and slid them up her spine and through her hair. She eased her mouth off of him.

"Take me inside of you. I need to feel you now, baby. Please," he begged of her. It aroused her body, made her nipples tighten, and she lifted up just as the cool liquid penetrated her ass along with Caldwell's thick fingers.

"Oh," she moaned aloud and lifted her hips forward, feeling Monroe's cock tease her pussy lips.

"Oh my God."

Max grabbed her cheeks as he returned to the bed, naked and in control.

"Didn't I tell you to ride Monroe, honey? Poor guy is bursting from the seams," Max said then kissed her deeply.

She reached under her and grasped Monroe's cock, sliding lower, taking him up into her cunt.

Behind her Caldwell stroked a finger in her ass. It was too much as she came, shaking all over.

"Hot damn you're so responsive. You're a damn dream, baby. A fucking fantasy come true," Max said after pulling from her mouth.

Her lips parted and she moaned, feeling Monroe thrust upward to her womb.

She adjusted her hips as her ass hung over the bed.

"You're so fucking tight, baby. Let me in, honey. Come on now," Monroe coaxed her as he held her hips and tried thrusting upward.

She was trying to hold back. She didn't want to explode again, but amazingly she felt another one coming.

"Oh God I can't take it."

Smack.

"Oh!" Caldwell smacked her ass and she came hard. She shook and moaned and lost that last bit of control she had.

"Holy God she came again. She's so fucking hot," Caldwell said and then he pulled his fingers from her ass.

He kissed her neck and shoulder.

"I'm coming in, baby. Get ready to come again for us."

He pressed her back a little lower as Max gripped her hair and cheeks.

She felt the tip of Caldwell's cock press against her anus. She moaned again and locked gazes with Max.

"Ours. All fucking ours. No one else ever. Right, Alicia?" Max asked, teeth clenched and desire and hunger in his eyes.

"Yes. Yes only you three ever."

"Fuck yeah," Caldwell said and gripped her hips and slid into her ass. Max kissed her deeply then pulled back and lowered her head to his cock. Monroe thrust upward as Caldwell pulled out to the tip of his cock. In and out they penetrated her and she could hardly focus, but Max gripped her hair and spoke to her, guided her along the way.

"Ease those muscles. Let go and feel. Feel us possess every part of you. You're a natural submissive, baby. You need us to protect you, care for you, and make love to you claiming every inch," Max said.

"Every fucking inch. Fuck she's so tight." Caldwell moaned aloud.

She suckled on Max's cock, easing her head up and down, finding her own rhythm.

"That's it, baby. Just like that. That feels so good. What a sexy, naughty girl you are. Fuck that feels incredible. Faster, baby. Make me come. Suck my cock and swallow my cum," Max told her as he caressed her hair, pinching her nipples while his brothers moved faster behind her and underneath her. It was so wild she was perspiring and losing focus when Max tightened up and gripped her hard. She felt the pull to her hair and it didn't scare her but aroused her. Made her feel like she had the ability to make big, bad, in-charge Max come undone. She suckled harder as he came, calling her name.

When he pulled from her mouth she gasped for air just as Caldwell thrust balls deep in her ass.

She cried out and rocked backward, which earned her a series of slaps to her ass from Caldwell. The burning only turned her on more and she countered their thrusts.

"Damn I'm there. Damn it," Caldwell said and shoved deep and came. She moaned and felt her body tighten. She was almost there. Just a few more strokes.

Caldwell pulled out and Monroe took over. He rolled her to her back, raised her thighs over his shoulders, and fucked her deeply.

"Oh God. Oh God I'm coming, Monroe. I feel it," she panted.

"Come with me, Alicia. Come now," he ordered as he thrust so fast and so deeply she cried out as she came. She thought she lost focus and maybe even her hearing as she screamed his name.

He rocked a few more times and she knew he came with her. He cupped her cheeks and lifted slightly, letting her legs lower to his sides and he kissed her deeply. She ran her fingers through his hair and hugged him when he released her hips as she straddled his waist.

"Mine. All fucking mine, forever," he said, sucking against her neck then her collarbone and to her breast. He pulled on her nipple and she moaned softly, her body so sensitive she felt limp and weak.

He continued to kiss her, suckling on her nipples and along her belly then ribs and hipbone. When he sucked hard on her groin she gasped and gave him a smack.

"Monroe," she reprimanded. He gripped her wrists and brought them to his mouth. He kissed them then held her gaze.

"I can't resist, you're so damn edible. I want every inch of you."

"Baby, I think you better get comfortable, we're going to keep you in this bed for quite some time," Max said, caressing her calf.

Caldwell chuckled.

"Give me a few minutes and I'll be ready for that pussy next."

"Caldwell," she reprimanded and covered her eyes with her arm. The men started tickling her and she laughed until she was totally exhausted and hoarse. She closed her eyes and they cared for her, washing her up then sliding into bed next to her and cuddling tight. She could live life like this feeling loved and content forever. That funny sensation hit her gut as concern raced through her mind, but with her three men cuddling, kissing, and loving her, it soon disappeared and exhaustion had her closing her eyes and dreaming of Caldwell, Monroe, and Max, loving them forever.

Chapter 7

"Okay spill the beans now, woman," Mercedes said to Alicia as she joined them for lunch at Fiona's restaurant located next to Spencer's dance hall.

Marlena chuckled as Alicia's cheeks turned a nice shade of pink and she played with her wine glass. "There's nothing to spill. The job at the Gordons's residence went very well."

"Honey, by the way you're smiling I'd say you got lucky triple time," Adele teased and they all started hooting and hollering, drawing attention to their table.

Alicia smiled and leaned back in her seat, brought her wine glass to her lips, and took a slow sip.

"Maybe," she said and Mercedes fist pumped into the air.

"Yes," she exclaimed.

"Look at you. Whatever happened I hope they keep it up. You look happy and a bit more confident," Adele pointed out.

"She does look good and definitely more confident," Marlena teased.

"Sex can do that for a woman. Isn't that right, Marlena?" Mercedes teased and they all laughed.

"A lady does not kiss and tell," Marlena said and winked at Alicia.

"That's always the response from a woman who's getting some. Damn, I'm jealous. I need to find a man," Mercedes stated aloud.

"You could have your choice, Mercedes, working in the sheriff's department surrounded by some of the hottest men around Chance," Adele said.

"Says the woman who works for three sexy, hot brothers she has yet to sleep with."

"Hey, I want to be more than just some roll in the hay or a servant in the office and out of it, thank you very much."

"Keep telling yourself that, Adele," Mercedes teased.

"Let's get back to Alicia. I want details. How did it happen? Where did they kiss you first?" Marlena asked.

"Did you do them in their wine room or did they taste you on the wine-tasting table?" Mercedes asked and Alicia shook her head and widened her eyes.

"The wine-tasting table," both Marlena and Adele said at the same time and they all started laughing.

"Cool it. I never said that," Alicia said.

"You didn't have to. It was written all over your face," Mercedes said and fanned herself.

"My God, look at you, girl. You go. You so deserve good men that are going to take care of you and treat you right. If they do anything to hurt you, you better tells us so we can kick their butts," Mercedes said and they all raised their glasses and cheered.

"What's this about kicking butts?"

Marlena gasped as Danny and Jack appeared. Jack placed his hands on Marlena's shoulders and her friends laughed.

Mercedes smiled. She was so happy for Marlena and for Alicia, too. She couldn't help but be envious.

"What are you two doing here?" Marlena asked them.

"We heard that you ladies were here enjoying dinner and that maybe you were headed to Spencer's next. Is that right?" Danny asked.

"All depends?" Mercedes said to them.

"Depends on what?"

"Are the drinks on the house?" she teased and the girls started laughing and cheering.

Marlena shook her head. "You fell right into that one."

Jack smiled. "No problem, you're a bunch of lightweights. How much could you possibly drink?" he said and Marlena smiled.

"Something tells me we'll all be calling in late tomorrow for work," Adele said and they all cheered.

* * * *

Alicia was feeling a buzz and knew she needed to stop drinking. She never got drunk in her life and she sure didn't want to now. Apparently Jack and Danny were concerned because a group of guys were coming onto Alicia and the girls, flirting and buying them drinks. Two of the guys were hitting on Alicia and she was telling them that she wasn't interested.

"You got a boyfriend or something?" the one guy asked.

"She's got three, buddy, I'd take a hike," Mercedes said and then winked.

Alicia chuckled.

The guy went to touch her hair.

"I don't see them here. If you were my woman, with this body, I wouldn't let you out of my sight," he told her.

"Well, I'm not your woman so leave me alone."

He reached out to touch her and Alicia saw the large hand and then heard the deep voice.

"Unless you want a broken arm I'd suggest you get the hell away from our woman immediately," Monroe told the guy and Alicia was shocked. The two guys immediately took off and Monroe stared down at her as Caldwell crossed his arms in front of his chest and seemed angry.

"Hi, Monroe, Caldwell. What are you doing here? Want a drink? Jack and Danny are buying," she told them, and her friends raised their glasses and cheered.

"I think you had enough, Alicia," Monroe told her as he took her hand and helped her up.

"Are we leaving?" she asked.

"I think we should."

"I'm leaving, guys. We'll do this again on Friday?" she said to her friends and they cheered.

"You'll make sure the others don't drive," Caldwell said to Jack.

"We've got it covered. Have fun," Jack said and chuckled. Alicia heard their exchange. They were worried about her friends and would ensure they all got home safely. That was Chance and the men who lived here. They cared and watched over women.

Once they got outside, the cool air collided against Alicia's cheeks. She opened her arms wide and turned in a circle.

"It's a beautiful night," she said, feeling her head spin a little. A strong arm wrapped around her waist.

"It sure is, but I think we should call it a night, baby," Monroe told her.

"Oh no, Monroe. It's too early," she told him and pressed him against his car. She laid her head against his chest.

"You guys are perfect. Are you for real?" she asked.

"Yes, baby, we are. Let's get you home."

"Wait, my home or your home?" she asked.

"Does it matter?"

She held his gaze and lost focus for a moment. "I never want to leave Chance. I never want to leave you, Caldwell, and Max."

Monroe cupped her cheeks and smile down at her.

"You won't have to."

She looked away and felt the tears in her eyes.

"He might make me if he comes here," she said and then stepped back.

* * * *

Caldwell went from angry at seeing two men hit on his woman to concerned at hearing what Alicia just said to them. Who would come take her from Chance, from them?

"Alicia, who are you talking about?" Monroe asked before he could.

She shook her head. She waved her hand in the air.

"It doesn't matter. I don't think I really care anymore. I think if you ever leave me and end it all, and even if Alvin is right and I'm used goods that no man will want, that at least I had happiness with the three of you."

Caldwell grabbed her shoulders and tuned her toward them.

"Who the hell is Alvin and when did he say such bullshit to you?" he asked.

She swallowed hard and looked utterly scared.

"Ease up, bro," Monroe told him. He shot him a look. He wondered how Monroe could be so calm after hearing what she just said. What else hadn't she told them?

She reached up and cupped Caldwell's cheek.

"It's okay, Caldwell, Alvin is my brother. He thinks I belong with Tony and will do anything he can to get us back together. But Tony's a controlling, lying cheater, who, like my brother, thinks I can't survive or succeed without them. They've held me down far too long. Besides, I've got you, Max, and Monroe in my corner. You won't hurt me like they did, right?" she asked then hugged Caldwell. Caldwell looked at Monroe.

"We'll ask tomorrow," he whispered and Caldwell nodded. Something wasn't right. Alicia hadn't told them everything about her ex or this brother of hers. What was going on? Would they come here looking for her or to cause trouble? He felt his defenses rise and protectiveness overwhelm him. Caldwell lifted her up into his arms as Monroe opened the door to the backseat.

"Come on, baby, we're taking you home."

* * * *

Amazingly Alicia awoke without a headache or much of a hangover. She was very thirsty and as her eyes focused on the room she not only saw she was not at her place, but in a very masculine setting and a bedside table that contained one large bottle of new water.

She eased herself up, noticing she was naked. She reached for the water, unscrewed the top, and began to drink. Once she ensured that her stomach was all right she thought about where she was and how Monroe and Caldwell came to get her at Spencer's. Then she tried to remember what they talked about on the way here to their house. She looked around the room noticing the king-size bed, the large windows, and the glass door that was currently ajar and sending a gentle breeze into the room. She looked around for her clothes and saw a man's shirt on the bed. Someone slept next to her last night. Was it Caldwell? She inhaled and caught the faint smell of his cologne. This must be Caldwell's room.

She pulled the shirt up and over her head then pulled back the sheets.

She walked toward the bathroom and freshened up, cleaned her eye makeup off and used her finger as a makeshift toothbrush, adding paste to it and scrubbing them then using mouthwash. Feeling a little bit better she brushed her hair, peeked around the corner to make sure no one was coming, and she used Caldwell's deodorant. Just in case. She quickly put it back into the drawer and headed back to the bedroom. She gasped when she saw Caldwell standing in the balcony doorway, leaning on the doorframe, shirtless and wearing boxers.

His arms were crossed in front of his chest and she felt a little ashamed. She never drank like she did last night. Not that she was drunk but she definitely had a good buzz going. Well maybe she was a little drunk considering she couldn't quite remember all of it.

"Are you feeling okay?" he asked her but didn't move toward her. She ran her fingers through her hair and looked down at the rug and how the shirt she wore, his shirt, lay past her knees. She glanced up at him.

"I'm a bit embarrassed. I don't ever drink like that. We were having such a good time and Jack and Danny weren't charging us for the drinks."

He uncrossed his arms and stalked toward her.

"So I should blame Jack and Danny for getting my woman drunk and letting guys hit on you?" he said and she took a retreating step backward until the backs of her thighs hit the bed.

"No, of course not, and no one was hitting on me. There was no one to blame, we were just letting off some steam." He reached out and gripped a handful of the shirt. She felt the cool air collide against her pussy under the material and she pulled her bottom lip between her teeth.

Caldwell's deep blue eyes bored into hers.

"We have some things to talk about, but first we need to take care of something."

She didn't know what he meant until he pulled her closer, leaned down, and kissed her deeply. She felt his erection press against her belly and she wrapped her arms around his waist. That kiss grew deeper quickly and soon he was pulling from her mouth, lifting the shirt up over her head, and tossing it to the floor. He stepped out of his boxers, his cock hard and long tapping against his belly as he pressed her down onto the bed.

He spread her thighs and swiped a finger to her already wet pussy. The man was lethal. A sex god and he wanted her.

She ran her fingers through his hair as his hot mouth landed on her breast. He suckled and pulled on her nipple and areola as she moaned with every stroke of his fingers. In and out he thrust fingers up into her cunt, arousing her, getting her ready for that thick, long muscle that pressed against her hipbone.

"You belong to my brothers and me. Last night when I saw those guys hitting on you, touching you, I almost lost it."

"No, Caldwell. They weren't going to do anything. I told them I wasn't interested."

"They saw that you had been drinking. Some guys see that as an opportunity to take advantage of a woman in that state. What if Monroe and I hadn't gotten there, or if Jack and Danny hadn't seen? Then what?" he asked very seriously.

She felt the tears fill her eyes. No one ever cared about her, about her safety or about men bothering her. She cupped his cheeks and held his gaze.

"But you were there. You stopped them from bothering me. No one has ever done that for me, or protected me."

He pulled his fingers from her pussy and he kissed her deeply. She felt his hands maneuver her thighs higher and the bulbous head pressed between her pussy lips. She widened her thighs, letting him in and Caldwell sunk into her pussy, wrapping his arms around her, burying her under his wide shoulders and muscular frame, and made love to her slowly, deeply.

He released her lips and kissed her neck, then ran his hands along her arms, down to her wrists, and clasped their fingers together as he raised her arms above her head.

He lifted his hips upward, thrusting, rocking his hips deeply into her, making her moan and gasp he felt so thick and hard.

Her breasts rocked and swayed as she held his gaze, got lost in the moment, in his blue eyes, and knew she loved him.

"You're mine, Alicia. Mine," he said and then began a series of hard, deep strokes that made her gasp and moan. He remained holding her hands, clasped together, united in body and in soul. She felt her body tighten as she shivered and tried to counterthrust, but Caldwell's cock was so deep inside of her, and he was so big in comparison that she couldn't move, she lost her breath and cried out his name.

"Come with me now. Come with me." He grunted and tightened up as she came and he did, too. They rocked together three more times and then he lowered over her, hugging her tightly, almost crushing her as he growled and then rolled to the side.

* * * *

He stroked her hair from her damp cheeks and then licked his lower lip. Their breathing calmed and he finally got rid of the barbaric feeling of possessiveness and needing to physically claim Alicia and mark her with his scent, his cock, and his cum. It was so carnal and wild but now that he'd made love to her and released his seed inside of her he felt more at ease. There were still questions to be answered and any minute his brothers would arrive to get answers, too. He just hoped that Max didn't turn it into an interrogation.

"Tell me about this brother of yours, Alvin?"

She tightened up and then looked away from him.

"Alvin?" she asked.

He placed his pointer and ring finger against her cheek and tilted her face back up toward him so he could look her in the eyes.

"Yes, Alvin. You mentioned him and your ex Tony last night. You said some things. Things that concerned Monroe, Max, and I."

"Max?"

"That's right. I want answers, too."

Max and Monroe entered the room. Max was in uniform.

She went to reach for the sheet to cover herself up but Monroe pushed the sheet away.

"No need for that. This all belongs to us. No one else," Monroe said and leaned down and kissed her hip bone. He ran a hand along her ass and squeezed it. Caldwell felt ready to claim her with his brothers again. That carnal need was getting worse.

"I understand you had a good time last night. You don't look hungover," Max said and crossed his arms in front of his chest. Yup, his brother was going to interrogate her. Caldwell needed to assist. The poor thing was shaking.

"I wasn't hungover because I wasn't drunk. Just buzzed a little," she said and looked away.

"That's not the way I heard it," Max said in that tone he used to get his point across.

"What did you hear?" she asked.

"That my woman was getting hit on by two men."

She lifted up and used her arm to cover her breasts.

"That's not fair. It wasn't my fault. Besides, I had it under control. I told them I wasn't interested."

Max stared at her.

He looked her body over.

"You belong to us. We're supposed to be the ones that protect you and watch over you. You can't be going out with friends and overdrinking. What if Danny and Jack hadn't called us? What if you were somewhere else that doesn't have men from Chance watching over you? Then what?" Max asked.

She knelt on the bed.

"Then I would do what I've done all my life, and depend on me and no one else."

Monroe placed his hand on her shoulder. She turned to look at him.

"That's not the case anymore, Alicia. You need to realize something very important. We're here for you. We're your protectors. You're not alone anymore," Monroe said then leaned forward and kissed her bare shoulder.

"We're not the asshole who lied to you, cheated on you, or told you that having sex with other men makes you used goods that no one wants."

"What?" she exclaimed.

"Last night you mentioned a brother, Alvin, and how he believes that you belong with your ex, Tony, and that you shouldn't be with any other men or Tony won't take you back because you'll be used goods."

She covered her mouth and looked at Caldwell then tried to get up off the bed.

Max pulled her toward him and kept his hands on her hips. She knelt in front of him.

"You need to tell us if you're still in love with this guy and if he's going to come here looking to take you back."

She shook her head side to side as Max's words sunk in and Caldwell was processing what Max said.

"I don't love him anymore."

"Your brother Alvin must think you do since he told you that you'd be used goods and that Tony won't take you back," Max pushed, and Caldwell let him. He was worried now, too, that they fell in love with Alicia and that she may still have feelings for her ex.

"Alvin is Tony's best friend. My brother has problems and he thinks that Tony is a means to financial freedom. But he also thinks that I belong to Tony and that I can't live, survive, succeed in anything without them. I don't love Tony. He hurt me. He lied to me and used me and he cheated on me. He sold the store out from under me."

"Then why is your brother trying to get you two back together? Why is he pushing this?" Monroe asked.

"Because Tony got money when he sold the business and he told us he reinvested it to make more. I haven't seen a cent of that money and never will. Tony is a liar and Alvin is holding on to him because he wants that money."

"Why haven't you just told them to leave you alone? Why are they still contacting you?" Max asked.

"Contacting you? Shit, you still talk to your ex and your brother after all that?" Caldwell couldn't help but to ask. It was like he needed clarification. Why would she talk to these men?

She lowered her head. "I haven't spoken to Tony recently. Only once since that day we made love for the first time."

"Go on," Max pushed.

She was silent as she sat back on her heels and moved her hair around her shoulders so it would cover her breasts.

"I know I shouldn't let them get to me. I know I should have told them to go to hell."

"But?" Max asked, tilting her chin up toward him so he could look her in the eyes.

She was crying and sniffling.

"I believed them," she said and at first Caldwell hadn't understood.

"You believed that you couldn't survive, work, or succeed without them like they told you?" Monroe asked in a tone that showed how shocked he was.

"I was weak, vulnerable, and so insistent upon making things right and keeping them happy and just wanting to be loved, that I let them walk all over me and make decisions for me."

"And what changed after the day we made love to you for the first time that you decided you wouldn't talk to them anymore?" Max asked her.

The tears rolled down her cheeks.

"The three of you showed me compassion, honesty, trust, and even an equality and worth that I never felt or experienced before. You asked me to trust you. You told me that you cared for me, would protect me and take away any pain and ensure that I would never feel pain again. I believed you."

Caldwell felt the shift from anger and confusion to adoration and love. Alicia trusted them with her heart and soul.

"That's right, Alicia. We're not Tony or Alvin. We're your men, your protectors and lovers. We're here for you and we're not going anywhere."

Max leaned forward and kissed her deeply. She wrapped her arms around his neck and held on tight.

His hand slid along her lower back then to her bare ass. Caldwell watched. His cock grew harder at the sight. She was sexy, beautiful, and she needed their love and protection. They had to find out more about these men and if they were coming to Chance.

"Baby, I need to ask you some more questions and I want honest answers," Max said.

She used the back of her arm to wipe her tears.

"Of course, Max."

He smiled.

"Where are Tony and Alvin right now?"

"Dallas."

"Since you aren't answering their phone calls would they come looking for you?"

She shook her head and looked away.

"Alicia, the truth.

She took a deep breath then released it.

"I don't know. I hope not."

Max looked pissed.

"You're to promise me, us, that if they contact you, or they show up in Chance that you are to call us, get in touch with one of us or our friends right away. Do you understand me?"

"Yes, Max. I promise."

"Good."

Max stepped back and began to undo his tie and then his belt with his gun and handcuffs and things.

"Now, I'm going to get undressed while you go undress Monroe and ride him. We're going to make love to you together, because we all need this right now. But know that you're going to get a nice spanking for being a naughty thing. Now climb on up there."

"A spanking?" she asked.

"Oh yeah, baby, a good one, too. They'll be no holding back information, or not letting us know that someone has hurt you or is bothering you, and certainly no going out drinking and not having one of us watching over you."

Max pulled off his shirt and stepped out of his pants.

"Don't keep Monroe waiting."

Caldwell looked at Max and he could tell that Max was worried. They would need to talk about this situation and come up with a plan just in case things were worse than Alicia may perceive.

Caldwell watched her climb up onto a very naked Monroe and kiss him deeply. Monroe maneuvered her around so that her ass was over the edge of the bed as she rode him. Alicia reached under and grabbed a hold of Monroe's cock and sunk her pussy down over him.

"Ahh, Alicia. It's heaven inside of you, baby." He pulled her down to kiss her as Max grabbed the lube.

He ran his hands along her ass and Alicia flinched, expecting her spanking to begin. Max was an expert at dishing out discipline, and it seemed especially the case for Alicia.

Caldwell ran his hands along his cock and crawled closer to Alicia.

She gasped the moment Max slapped her ass the first time. He watched as Max massaged where he slapped her ass and then he spanked the other side.

Alicia gasped again and then wiggled her hips. Monroe gripped her hips and shoved upward so his cock was deep in her pussy. That was when Max slapped her ass again and again then caressed away the burn.

Alicia moaned and shook.

"Fuck she's coming. Our woman likes a nice spanking, Max," Monroe told their brother.

"More than a cock in her ass?" Max teased then began to squeeze some lube into her ass before he thrust a finger then a second finger.

"Oh God, Max, please. Please."

Smack, smack, smack.

"Oh," she moaned aloud.

"It's coming, baby. You want more of this?" Max asked and began to thrust two fingers in and out of her ass as Monroe thrust up and down into her pussy.

"More. More, Max," she said and pushed back against his fingers.

Max leaned forward and nipped her ass cheek. One then the next and she shifted to the side he nipped.

He ran his hands along her thighs, spreading them wider. Then he pulled his fingers from her ass and leaned over her.

"You took your spanking like a good girl, now I've got your reward."

He aligned his cock with her anus and slowly began to push into her ass. Caldwell watched and leaned closer as he brushed her hair from her face and brought his cock to her lips.

She opened immediately, appearing hungry and needy for more cock.

Her warm breath hit his sensitive flesh. She moaned as Max thrust balls deep into her ass and then it began. In and out they stroked their cocks into their woman, claiming her, loving her, and conquering that savage need to claim what was rightfully theirs. As she willingly gave all of herself to them and accepted their dominance, he couldn't help but to feel that they were empowering her, too. They were building her confidence, daring her to succeed in all of her dreams and wishes, because they would back her up, protect her, and ultimately love her because she completed them like no one ever before.

* * * *

Alicia was getting dressed after her shower. She wanted to meet Caldwell and Monroe in town for lunch and then to go to the construction site to check out the process of the buildings. All the legal documents were signed and the three of them were partners in her business. They would hold her mortgage and she would pay them monthly. They couldn't sell the building without her okay and they would help her with advertising and promoting her work with the option of being full partners if things took off as they hoped.

She was feeling pretty damn good and she was going to meet their mom and dads tonight as well. She felt a little nervous as she slipped on her pretty pink skirt and camisole then slipped on her sandals. Things were great and would only get better.

She heard her cell phone ring and assumed it was Max. He was always checking up on her.

"Hello."

"Where the hell have you been? How come you haven't returned any of our calls?" Tony asked her, yelling into the phone.

She panicked and then the idea hit her.

"Oh, I moved and I'm going to be getting a new number, too, so there's no need to contact me ever again."

"What? You can't do that. What about Alvin? He's your brother."

"Well, you two seem to care so much about one another, you can take care of him and stay in touch with him. Good-bye, Tony, and good riddance." She disconnected the call and then she screamed out in joy and fist-pumped like Mercedes did all the time when she was excited and pumped.

She tossed the phone down and then thought about what she should do next. Call Max and tell him what she did? Get a new cell phone number? She thought about it. She was a different woman now. Thanks to Max, Caldwell, and Monroe. She didn't have to tell them about this phone call. Tony and Alvin were done as far as she was concerned. She moved on for the better, and they could go to hell.

She grabbed her purse and applied her lip-gloss. She was going to meet her men and be excited over her new store and all the work ahead of her. This was her dream and thanks to the love and support of Monroe, Max, and Caldwell, it was going to be a reality.

* * * *

"She did what?" Alvin asked as Tony filled him in on the phone call.

"She's seeing someone. I know she is," Tony said in anger.

"Who could she be seeing? She's weak and waiting on you."

"No, she isn't. Have you looked into that town where she was staying? It's not normal there. They do things there we're not used to and nor is Alicia. It's like a cult."

"What the hell are you talking about, Tony?"

"They share women there, Alvin. Two, three, four, even five men to one woman."

"What the hell? Are you serious? How long have you known this?"

"I just found out the other day. I've been debating about going there and talking to her. But I think we need to do something more drastic to save her."

"What do you mean?"

"I mean sneak in and take her out of there without the men who are trying to use her knowing. They'll have their way with her body. They'll do things to her and she'll never be the same woman again. I'm going to have to do this."

"Maybe it's too late? I mean if she is already involved in this type of thing then it could be over."

"It can't be over. I need her," Tony said and then looked at the documents on his desk. He needed Alicia's signature so he could get all the money for himself. He'd pushed off the lawyers for long enough. He had fun with other women and playing the field, but it was time to secure his treasure, cash in on the money invested. He needed her signature and consent and then he would send her off, but not before he took her one last time. If she liked three or four men fucking her at once then he would enjoy the time he had with her so she would never forget what she could have had with him.

He smiled to himself. She was weak and easily manipulated by him. The stupid woman loved him and all because he had her first.

"What do you need from me, Tony?"

"Don't worry about it, Alvin. I'll take care of everything like always."

* * * *

"I was thinking that maybe over here you could set up your studio so you get the rays of the sun, the natural light from across the way," Monroe told her as they walked around the construction site and what would be her storefront very soon.

"Plus, by having the corner unit, the largest one in the strip, you have access to additional windows where you can display your pieces," Caldwell added and pointed to the sidewall that was loaded with windows. She was so excited as she imagined her pieces on display, the natural light shining through them and reflecting around the room and into the street.

She walked toward Caldwell and hugged him tight. He caressed her lower back and then chuckled as the rumble tickled her skin that was against his chest.

"I think she likes it," he said to Monroe.

She felt the hand on her shoulder then the caress to her hair. She looked up into Monroe's eyes.

"I think she likes it, too."

She pulled from Caldwell and then hugged Monroe.

"Of course I love it. Who wouldn't?"

She pulled back and looked around the room. It was so big.

"What's wrong?" Max asked, standing there with his arms crossed in front of his chest.

She pulled her bottom lip between her teeth.

"It's very big. Do I really need all this space?"

"You will with a sitting area and coffee and snack bar over here," Monroe told her.

"What?" she asked.

"Don't you worry, we've got it covered," he added.

"People like to browse and shop, but they also want a reason to linger and get absorbed in your creations. They can sit here for quite some time in amazement of your work. So what better way to entice them in and make them stay and purchase your pieces then to provide gourmet coffees and locally made desserts?" Caldwell asked.

"I can't do that, too. There wouldn't be enough time and I can't afford to hire someone to do that right now, maybe months from now, and that's if this takes off. Oh God, this is too much. I don't think I can handle this." She started to panic. Literally panic as her chest tightened and she bent forward.

Max was by her side caressing her back.

"Easy, darling, it's going to be just fine. Monroe and Caldwell are in charge of the coffee bar and snack side of the business. You just enjoy making your creations."

She looked up and he pulled her against him, caressing her back and squeezing her ass.

"God, you're so beautiful when you're freaking out." He chuckled.

She squinted her eyes at him and gave his chest a light slap. He raised one of his eyebrows at her and she felt her ass cheeks warm and she lowered her eyes. He gave her ass a tap and chuckled.

"You're our woman and we're your men. We do what's best for you and what makes you happy and less stressed. We can't make those gorgeous creations you do, but we can help out on the business end. Monroe and Caldwell have this all covered. There's not a thing for you to worry about."

"But who will work there? Who pays for them and for the products and things needed? Is it really gourmet like lattes and espressos, biscotti and pastries?"

He squeezed her ass a little snugger, pulling her against him, making her thigh rise up against his thigh.

"You trying to take over the menu?" he teased.

She ran her hands up his chest and then pressed against him.

"I was just thinking what would go perfect."

She felt his fingers move under her skirt then one finger twirled around the string of her panties before pressing lower to her pussy.

"I know what would be perfect right now," he said, holding her gaze as she stared up into his eyes all dreamy like. She felt his thick finger push up into her needy cunt. She gripped his forearms.

"Max," she whispered.

"Open for me. Let me in so I can feel how aroused and needy for my cock you are, baby."

"Max, please. Someone might see," she said in a panic. They were on a construction site, although she hadn't seen any workers down this end since they pulled up in the cars.

"No one is going to see. This body belongs to us, no one else," Monroe said as he pressed up against her back.

"Lean back on me. Let yourself go. I've got you. Always," Monroe said.

She did as they told her because she trusted them. Hell, she loved them.

Gripping onto Max's uniform shirt on his arms and leaning her back and shoulders against Monroe, she opened for Max. Felt his thick fingers thrusting, curling, and coaxing the orgasm building inside of her.

Caldwell unbuttoned her top, unclipped her bra, and leaned forward to feast on her nipple and breast.

She rocked her hips, could feel Monroe's hard erection behind her, and she knew they would head to their place after this and make love, unless of course she would allow them to fuck her right here on the construction site. She realized she didn't even care. She never felt so needed, so hungry for sex and for that deep connection ever. They could take her right here. She was wearing a skirt. All they had to do was replace fingers with cocks and she would be in heaven.

"Max," she gasped, feeling the pinch to her clit and the stroke to her pussy.

"I thought I was boring you."

She shook her head.

"No. Never."

"What were you thinking about?" Caldwell asked as he held her snugly around the waist under her breasts with one arm and used his other hand to massage her ass.

"I was thinking about making love to the three of you right here. How you could lift my skirt and take me any way you wanted.

"Monroe," she gasped when she felt him nip her nipple.

"And what if someone walked in here? What if a bunch of construction guys walked in on us fucking our woman?" he asked.

"You'd protect me. You'd never let that happen."

"Ah hell," Max exclaimed and pulled back.

She didn't know what was happening until Caldwell turned her around and began to give orders.

"Hands on the counter, spread your legs," he said.

Her heart was racing as she pressed her hands onto the wooden counter, feeling the sawdust hit her palms and the smell of freshly cut wood tickle her senses. Before she could absorb it all, hard hands gripped her hips, pulling them back and wider, then a moment later, thick, hard cock filled her to her womb.

She cried out.

Max grabbed her cheeks.

"Shh, baby, this is really dangerous, but you got us all horny and ready for your pussy right here in our place. This is one hell of a way to christen your storefront." He covered her mouth and kissed her as Caldwell thrust into her so hard and so fast she moaned her first orgasm.

She felt on fire, like she was naughty and about to get caught being fucked by three men on a construction site.

"Oh God this is wild. Harder, Caldwell. Harder, I need you," she said.

He grabbed her ass cheeks, spread them wider, and thrust balls deep into her pussy until he came with a grunt.

He pulled out so damn fast she felt her head spin. Before she could stretch her legs, Monroe was there and pressing his cock into her pussy next. He suckled her neck and cupped her breasts that were bobbing and swaying from his hard, deep strokes. She absorbed the smell of sex, combined with that sawdust, fresh paint, and her men's cologne. She was hot, excited, and came again.

"Holy fuck she's so turned on right now. You like not knowing if someone is watching us fuck you right now? You like the idea of possibly getting caught with our dicks in your cunt and your body exposed?" Max asked her.

"Yes," she cried out.

Smack, Smack, Smack.

"Max," she exclaimed, and Monroe came and grunted against her neck.

He pulled out and there was Max, grabbing her by the hips and pulling them back so only her palms were on the counter in front of her.

He slapped her ass again.

"You're a naughty little thing. Goddamn but it turns me on like nothing else. What do you need from me, Alicia?" he asked as he caressed her ass cheeks, swiped the cream from her pussy to her anus, and pressed into her ass.

"Your cock, Sheriff. I need it now."

"Oh fuck," Caldwell moaned. She saw him retucking in his shirt and then she felt Monroe caressing her hair back.

"Here I come, baby," Max said and he aligned his cock with her pussy and shoved in deep. She gripped the counter and from there on out she barely caught a full breath. Max fucked her hard, fast, and the sounds of their flesh slapping against one another echoed in the store. She would never forget making love to them here.

"You're ours forever, Alicia. We're in this together. One unit, one family. Forever," he growled out. He cupped her breasts with his big hard hands and he thrust his hips so damn fast she cried out her release and then he grunted his. He shivered behind her then kissed her neck, squeezed her tight, and whispered against her neck. "I love you, baby. That's what this is. Love."

The tears rolled down her cheeks as he pulled from her pussy. She turned around and hugged him tight. "I love you, too. I love all of you," she said.

"We love you," Monroe added and kissed her cheek.

"I love you, too, baby, but we need to get you presentable. I think we're pushing this a little too far and I don't want anyone seeing my woman's pussy, tits, and ass," Caldwell said.

Max chuckled and Alicia felt her cheeks warm as Max set her down and he fixed his pants and uniform.

She felt Monroe's hands against her ass and waist as he helped her put on her panties and fix her skirt. Caldwell reclipped her bra and then buttoned the blouse after he fixed the camisole.

They stepped back.

"How do I look?" she asked as she smoothed her hands down her skirt. Meanwhile her legs felt like Jell-O and she felt a little light-headed.

"Like our sexy little woman. Come on, we're starving now," Max said to her and Monroe and Caldwell chuckled.

She looked around the store one last time feeling like she was going to succeed and like she would be happy for once in her life and she would be sharing it with three men she loved and adored.

She hugged Max's arm as they exited the building.

Monroe caressed her ass.

"Two more minutes and we would have been busted," Monroe said and she saw the construction crew walking down the sidewalk toward them. Her cheeks heated.

"I don't know, Monroe, I think the three of you could have lasted a few more minutes."

"Ouch." Caldwell pinched her ass and she jumped. The men chuckled.

"Watch yourself, Alicia, or they'll be a nice long spanking when we get home and I can assure you walking will be a task," Max said then brought her knuckles to his lips and kissed them. She saw his expression go from intense and hard to sweet and teasing. She smiled.

"I don't know, Sheriff, I'm kind of getting used to your spankings and I think I like them."

"Oh brother, she's turning into a monster," Monroe said.

"I think some changes in the bedroom might be in order," Caldwell said.

"Don't worry, I've got my handcuffs, and I know how to use them."

Her eyes widened and she wasn't sure if she should be scared or aroused. When she got into Caldwell's car with assistance from the sheriff and the feel of his handcuffs brushing along her hip, her body reacted.

She was definitely interested in being handcuffed by her sheriff. The idea of it had her closing her mouth and sitting quietly in the backseat.

"I'll meet you at the restaurant," Max said and winked. Monroe and Caldwell held firm expressions that only added to her arousal. Oh God these three men had changed her life, her perspective on the future and what love was really all about. They told her they loved her. She smiled wide and never felt happier in her life. Everything was perfect, for once in her life.

* * * *

He was shaking with anger. She was nothing but a fucking whore, allowing three men, including the local sheriff, to fuck her on a construction site. Fuck! The sight of her pleased expression and the way she caressed them, enticed them with her body, a body that belonged to him, really fucking pissed him off.

Tony slammed his hand against the wall. He thought he might get caught. Hell, he wanted to ruin their little fuck fest and demand they get their dicks out of his woman's cunt. He was furious, jealous, worried that her involvement with a lawman could screw things up. He needed to think and do it quickly. Alicia had to sign the papers and not read them. She would know that she was giving up two hundred thousand dollars to him. The stupid bitch. He needed a better plan. Those men were big. They looked important and obviously she fucked them into helping her get another storefront. She was not so weak and stupid as he thought. He needed to be smarter. He'd get her and take care of business. He just needed to avoid those three assholes.

* * * *

"It's so nice to finally meet you in person, Alicia. God, you're so beautiful," Sianne said to Alicia as Max, Caldwell, and Monroe shook their dads' hands after they introduced Alicia to them and to Mom.

Max watched the two women embrace and smile. Over the past few weeks they talked on Skype whenever their mom touched base. Truth was, their mom loved Alicia's work and wanted to see the progress she made. Sianne was involved with different galleries in Austin and even New York and California. She had connections and it seemed she was really interested in Alicia's talent.

"So tell me about how you got started doing the stained glass. Did someone teach you? Did you take classes?" Sianne asked.

"I'm actually self-taught. I used to read about how stained glass windows and other things were made in Europe and centuries ago. It caught my interest and I would pick up books on them and then of course techniques in making stained glass art. I loved it and it just came natural to me."

"Well, I have to say that I love your work, too. I know a lot of people in Austin who own galleries. I was showing off your piece you did for my sons and they loved it. They're very interested in seeing more pieces. Do you have a portfolio of some sort?"

"I do. They really liked it?" Alicia asked and Max couldn't help but smile. She was so shy, so humble about her abilities. She was simply glowing and he couldn't help but think their lovemaking only an hour ago on the construction site and the fact he told her he loved her brought it on.

"Wow, I'd never think we'd see the day," Colonel, his father, whispered to him. His other dads, Walt and Brook, chuckled.

"What's that?" he asked and Monroe and Caldwell stared at their dads, too.

"The three of you in love. Especially you, Max."

"Really?" Max asked and their dads chuckled.

"Don't get on the defensive. I'm only teasing. I can remember a certain young blonde who snagged my attention and brought out the kindness in me," Colonel said and looked at his wife.

"Yup. Softened him up. People started getting away with warnings instead of tickets," Brook teased and they chuckled. Max took over as sheriff for Chance five years ago after an election. It had been anonymous and the town was thrilled with keeping the position in the family. He glanced at Alicia. He could keep his same personality with the public and as the sheriff of the town, but with Alicia, he was a different man. She brought out something in him he didn't even recognize. It had to be love. Staring at her as everyone conversed around them, he couldn't help but feel worried. He had a big responsibility. To this town, to the people, to his brothers, Alicia, and his family. Having Alicia made things different. He felt even more protective of those he loved, but he also wanted a bit of what he protected and witnessed in Chance. The love and connection of family, of children, and having a wife.

"She'll make a good wife, Max. You and your brothers be sure not to wait too long. As Sheriff of this town you're in the spotlight. You're a leader of how things should be done. Keep the traditions. Be strong and be honest, and everything will work out perfectly," Colonel said and squeezed his son's shoulder.

He nodded his head. It seemed his brothers and he had some planning to do.

Chapter 8

Alicia was exhausted. She had been working on her stained glass artwork determined to have several dozen pieces on display for the store opening in another month. She left the men's home late this morning after spending the night with them and talking about color schemes and how Monroe and Caldwell were negotiating with a large coffee and franchise place to get them interested in setting up shop in Alicia's store. They were going all out for her and she loved them for it. Every time she thought about them she felt her heart lift with joy and her belly feel like butterflies were in it. They were so amazing and she wondered how she had gotten so lucky. Then of course their mom had those connections with galleries and it seemed they were interested in her work. She went from a nobody, struggling to make ends meet, to someone important, someone loved. She smiled as she adjusted her shoulder bag and walked up the stairs to her apartment above the garage.

She couldn't wait to shower and hit bed. She had been going on empty for days now and it was getting to her. One good night sleep and she should be good for the weekend.

She turned the knob on her door and chastised herself for the dozenth time about locking her door. Max would be so pissed off at her. She felt her cheeks warm. He would give her a spanking. She liked those.

As she entered the room she reached for the switch to turn on the lights. Nothing happened. Confused, and never having an issue before, she walked further into the room, dropping her bag and reaching for the lamp by the table. It didn't work either. She realized too late that something was terribly wrong.

She heard the click of the gun and turned around, gasping.

She couldn't breathe. Her chest hurt and she was so shocked she stepped backward. "Tony? What are you doing here?"

"Tying up some loose ends, you little slut." The strike to her jaw with the butt of the gun came so fast she couldn't duck. She fell to the rug, holding her jaw, only for him to press the gun to her throat.

"You stupid bitch. After all I did for you and you cheat on me with three men? Three?"

"Tony, why are you here? You left me. You cheated on me," she cried. He struck her again and she felt her lip split.

"Get up. You're coming with me."

"No. No, I'm not going anywhere." He grabbed her by her hair. He was stronger than her, much bigger, and she had never seen him so irate. She had to do something. No one would know that Tony took her. She had to fight him.

She tried pulling from his hold and he struck her again and again. She couldn't focus. Her eye instantly swelled and her ribs felt so sore.

"Get up and cooperate, or your boyfriends will suffer."

"What? How?" she asked, slowly getting up and knocking over the lamp. When someone came looking they would know there was trouble, a break-in, and they would send help. She had to be smart. Tony obviously lost his mind.

He grabbed her hair and shoved her to the door. He held the gun to her side. She looked to the distance. Lights were still on at Dr. Anders's place, but Lisa Marie was pregnant. She didn't want her or the baby to get hurt. She couldn't make a sound. They had children in the house. She had to cooperate and wait for a better opportunity.

Tony shoved her into her car. "You drive," he told her and she started the car, pulled out, hands shaking, eye so swollen she could hardly see between that and the tears rolling down her cheeks. She ached everywhere. As they headed out of the driveway, down the dirt road and to the main roadway, she felt the hand on her thigh moving under her skirt. She slowed the car down and kicked at his hands.

"Don't touch me."

He pressed the gun to her neck and eased against her. His fingers grazed her panties and she tried pressing her thighs together but he forced his hand between her legs. She cried out. "Don't touch me. What do you want from me?"

"What you've been giving up to those three dicks. We're going to have some fun, Alicia. Now that I know you're not so fragile and like a cock in every hole."

She gasped.

He caressed her jaw then ran his hand down her blouse and over her breast.

"I saw you fucking them."

She glared at him and then back at the road. "That's right. On the construction site. Looks like you played them well. You getting your own store?"

"Fuck you," she spat at him. He chuckled and her anger grew.

"I've got some papers for you to sign. Then you can go do whatever you want whoring your body out to three men. You know they don't give a shit about you."

"They love me and I love them." She raised her voice and he slammed her head so hard it hit the side of the window and she lost control of the car a moment. He grabbed the wheel.

"Focus. We've got a short time to get this done."

She was crying, feeling dizzy and in pain as she tried to focus on the road.

"What do you want?"

"Your signature on some papers and…"

She felt his hand ease between her legs again.

"One last screw, and nothing is off limits. After all, I was your first. How did your men feel about that? Or didn't you tell them the truth?"

She stepped on the gas and began going faster. Hatred filled her gut and she wanted Tony dead, gone, and out of her life. Things were perfect. Everything was going great and he was going to destroy it all. She wouldn't let him touch her. She wouldn't sign ay papers for him. She was done with him, with feeling this pain and being used.

"Slow down before a cop sees you," he yelled.

"Are you afraid, Tony?" she asked and he wedged the gun against her throat. She slowed the car down.

"I'm not afraid of anything. In fact, I'll fuck you then kill you so you can never see your men again. How's that for scared? Now drive. We're limited on time. Usually those men are always with you. Their mistake and my good luck. Drive."

Alicia felt the tears rolling down her cheeks. She was shaking now. The fight within her was weakening. He had a gun. He would do like he said and rape her then kill her. She would never see Caldwell, Max, and Monroe again. Why had she ever fallen for his charms? Why?

* * * *

Max was in the office. It was getting late and he wished he could head home to Alicia, but she was stressing out and trying to get pieces ready for the shop when it opened. He smiled. They kept her occupied this afternoon when they all met for lunch at their place. An hour break had turned into two hours, and he was ready to say screw it and stay with her in bed. He talked to his brothers about how difficult it was leaving her at night. They were getting angry about not holding her in their arms in bed every night and about how more changes needed to be made, but she had so much going on. He didn't want to overwhelm her by asking her to move in with them. They were with each other more often than not. In fact, tonight was the first time in weeks that one of them wasn't with her. It gave him anxiety as he finished up his work and prepared to leave the office. Maybe he should stop by to make sure she was okay?

He smiled to himself as his cell phone began to ring. It was Caldwell calling.

"Hey, bro, what's going on? How did the meeting go?"

"It went great. We have awesome news for Alicia. Is she with you?"

"No. I'm still in the office. I was just getting ready to leave."

"Her car isn't by the side of the garage, and there aren't any lights on in the apartment. Wait, Monroe is going up to check it out. So listen to this, we talked with the CEO of the company and he wants in. Thinks the location is great and sees the potential for growth and income. Plus, we worked it out so that Alicia gets paid for use of the building and the traffic. By the terms he placed on the table, she'll be getting a nice monthly income that not only will pay her mortgage but also give her a nice nest egg for retirement. We're going to hook her up with our financial guys next week. God, I can't wait to tell her."

Max smiled. Alicia would be thrilled. His brothers were really looking out for her on the financial end. It made him feel more protective of her and like his responsibility would be protection, security, and love.

"What?" Caldwell yelled.

"What's going on?" Max asked. He could hear the concern in Caldwell's voice.

"Shit, Max, Monroe said that the electricity is out in Alicia's apartment. There's things knocked over. He thinks someone broke in."

"What? I'm on my way. I'm calling it in. Don't touch anything."

Max stood up and grabbed his keys. As he headed to the door he saw some of the deputies on break and a few others coming in and out.

"Who's out on Blanchard or in the vicinity?" he asked.

"Deputy Taylor Dawn should be. What's going on, Max?" Deputy Williams asked and he explained.

"We're on it. What do you need us to do?"

"Keep me posted of any suspicious activity. Put out an APB on Alicia's car."

He headed out of the building, his gut twisting and turning as he thought about what could be going on. He didn't feel right and instantly he thought about Alicia's ex-boyfriend and her brother. He called into the station.

"I need you to also look up these individuals and find out where they are. Have the local police departments send someone to their residence to see if they're home and to question them."

"Who are they, Max?" Williams asked.

"Tony is Alicia's ex-boyfriend and the other is her brother. Both are trouble and could have something to do with this. It's the only lead I've got."

"I'll take care of it."

Max got to Alicia's to find two other deputies there already and Monroe and Caldwell looking very pissed off. He got out of the patrol truck.

"What do you have, Taylor?" he asked the deputy.

"Definitely suspicious. Looks like a struggle took place in the living room by the front door."

"We've got cut utility wires in the back," Deputy Harris added as he came around the front with a flashlight.

"Son of a bitch. Anyone could have her," Monroe said.

"I had Williams put out an APB on her vehicle and also find out where Tony and Alvin live and get some patrol units over to question them."

"You think her ex showed up or her brother and did this?" Caldwell asked.

"I don't know what's going on but that's all we have as possibilities right now. Nothing like this has ever happened in town before. No break-ins, no abductions by strangers. Well, except for the Marlena situation and that was resolved. So I have to cover all the bases I can think of right now, Caldwell."

"Fuck. What if it is him? What if her ex came here to take her back?" Monroe asked.

"Then from the looks of the apartment she put up a fight," Taylor said.

The radio went off and Max answered.

"Where?" he asked. "I'm on my way."

"Someone reported a speeding vehicle heading toward the construction site on the edge of town. They believe it was Alicia's."

"Let's go. We can get there in five minutes."

Caldwell and Monroe jumped into Max's truck and the other deputies followed in their vehicles. He prayed that Alicia was okay and that they got to her in time. He didn't know what her ex was capable of, but obviously he had been watching her and waiting for an opportunity. Why was he bringing her to the constructions site?

* * * *

Alicia headed into the construction area too fast. Tony yelled about slowing down and not being able to see. She didn't care what happened to her, she wasn't letting Tony touch her and make her sign papers. She turned the wheel, making a hard right, and didn't see the debris in the way. The vehicle lifted and bumped up and down as she hit the brakes, spun out, and then crashed into the machinery. She felt her neck jerk hard and her forehead hit the steering wheel. Stunned, she smelled and saw through smoke coming from her car and glanced at Tony. He was holding the side of his head. The gun wasn't in his hands. She tried opening the door and it wouldn't budge. She started climbing out of the window. She needed to get as far away from Tony as she could.

As she began descending toward the dirt she felt the hands on her legs and heard him yelling.

"Not so fast. I've got you. You can't get away from me."

She kicked at him, heard the grunt, and then fell to her knees. She landed against the front tire and the debris cutting her side but she didn't care. She needed to run. She headed toward the construction site and by the buildings. It was dark. So dark she couldn't see a thing as she banged into something, knocking over tools or nails.

"You can't run, Alicia. I'm going to finish what I started," he yelled at her and she was shaking with fear. Could he see her? She couldn't see him. She reached out with her hands, her fingers hitting cold concrete and the openings of unfinished windows. She lowered down, thinking if she kept her back against the wall that she would see him coming if he charged. She continued to scoot around and could hear him getting closer.

In the distance she heard the sirens and she knew they were coming. Somehow Max and the others knew she was in danger. She waited to make her move when the light came upon her. Tony held his cell phone at her with one hand and the gun pointed at her with the other.

"I win," he said, and she took a deep breath and ran to the right.

The construction site filled with lights and the sound of gunshots went off around her. She screamed and tried running through the buildings when she felt the sharp pain to her shoulder. She fell forward, hitting her face on the concrete and then feeling the hands on her, ripping her top and turning her over. She couldn't move her arm as she tried fighting Tony off with one hand.

He was striking her when suddenly another gunshot went off. Tony instantly stopped ripping her clothes and fell to the side. Men grabbed him, handcuffing him as flashlights illuminated her body and her face.

"Jesus, baby. Oh God we need an ambulance. She's been shot," Caldwell yelled out. Him and Monroe looked at her and checked her over carefully.

"That fucking bastard. Is he dead, Max? Did you kill that fucker for what he did to her?" Monroe yelled.

"He's alive. He'll suffer every day for the rest of his life. I'll make sure of it," Max said as he looked at her.

Alicia was shaking and crying. "How did you find me? How did you know something was wrong?" she asked as Monroe pulled off his shirt and applied pressure to the gunshot wound on her shoulder.

"We were coming to tell you some good news. We couldn't wait until tomorrow, baby," Caldwell said and caressed the dirt from her cheeks.

"Thank God we did. When we saw your apartment and realized someone broke in we were so scared. Max figured out it was your ex. What the hell happened?" Monroe asked her.

"I hurt everywhere. My shoulder is throbbing," she cried.

* * * *

Max felt sick.

"We'll talk about it later. The ambulance is here. You're safe now, Alicia. We've got you," Max told her as the paramedics moved them out of the way.

Max watched in horror as their friends tended to her injuries. Her clothes were ripped. Her ex abducted her, beat her, shot her, and tried to rape her. He felt sick, angry, and he wanted answers.

"You guys take care of Alicia. I'm getting down to the bottom of this situation with her ex and what he wanted. The man is going to pay for this."

"You should come to the hospital. Let someone else deal with it," Caldwell told him.

Max shook his head. He felt responsible. He should have been with her. One of them should be with her at all times. That was what she deserved and needed.

"No, I want this resolved, and the only way to ensure that this asshole keeps away from her is to make sure he goes to jail for a very long time. I'll get to the hospital. You two take care of her and watch over her."

Chapter 9

"She's my sister. I'm her family and you have no right to keep me from seeing her," Alvin yelled as Deputy Taylor Dawn held him back. Max pointed at Alicia's brother.

"You're not her brother. If you were her brother then you never would have said the things you did to her to break her down and make her feel weak and incapable of surviving without you and that asshole who tried to kill her."

"I didn't have anything to do with what Tony did to her or how he tried to kill her. That's why I'm here so I can see her. I was so worried."

Max wasn't sure what to do. Every gut instinct in his body told him this guy was a laying sack of shit.

"Oh really?" Caldwell said as he approached along with some of their friends. Locals in the community, including a lawyer friend of theirs who helped Max earlier. Through many connections they were able to find out some concrete information to put Tony behind bars.

Caldwell read from his phone.

"I have some information here that proves you've been working with Tony to get Alicia to sign papers handing over all funds to Tony and nothing to her."

"I did no such thing," Alvin protested.

"Sure you did. You're signature is on this piece of paper indicating that Tony planned on giving you a cut just for helping him make your sister believe his story," the lawyer said.

"He was going to give you five thousand dollars. That's it. The store front sold for two hundred thousand. Tony screwed you too." Caldwell added.

Alvin's eyes widened and then he became irate.

"That stupid bitch had to come to Chance and met you assholes. If she just signed the damn papers none of this would have happened."

"Get him out of here," Caldwell yelled.

"Wait," Max said and approached Alvin.

"You're nothing but a lowlife loser who could have had a great relationship with your only family member, a complete sweetheart who would have done anything for you. Instead you belittled her. You hurt her and for that I give you this one final warning. If you ever try to contact Alicia, try to talk to her, make any kind of contact with her whatsoever, my brothers and I will personally see to it that you go to jail for a very long time."

Alvin looked at him like he didn't believe a word he said. Max raised one of his eybrows at him. He grabbed the front of Alvin's shirt in a fist and looked down into the weasel's eyes. He was shaking.

"You think I'm bluffing? Let's just say my brothers and I have connections, and we may or may not have documented proof of you laundering money, cashing fake checks and stealing and using credit cards. So I suggest you disappear. Because if you ever set foot in Chance, in any surrounding states near South Carolina, my brothers and I will personally deal with you. Alicia is our woman, we love her and we will do anything and everything possible to keep her safe and happy. You got it?"

Max asked as he abruptly released the front of Alvin's shirt.

Alvin nodded his head.

"Now you can take out the trash." Monroe told Taylor.

"My pleasure," Taylor replied and took Alvin out of the waiting room and out of their sight.

Max exhaled then ran his hand over his mouth. He couldn't wait to get to Alicia and to tell her that she didn't have to worry anymore.

He and his brothers with the help of friends in town and lawyers got the money back that Alicia deserved for selling her part of the business in Dallas. Her ex had conned her, and apparently her brother, who showed up at the hospital claiming to not know anything about Tony's plans. However, further investigation into her brother Alvin proved that he was to get thirty percent of the two hundred thousand dollars Tony tried to take from Alicia. Now that money was in an escrow account for safe keeping until Alicia was ready to deal with it.

* * * *

The last three weeks had been difficult. Alicia was depressed and trying to work on healing her shoulder so she could prepare for the store opening. They'd postponed it until next week. The doctors said she was healing fine, but Max felt it was psychological with Alicia. Her abduction, assault, and being used and lied to by Tony and her own brother had gotten to her. Sometimes he would catch her staring off and wiping tears from her eyes. Their mom was a huge help, encouraging Alicia and making her feel like part of the family. Max knew it would take some time but he hoped she realized soon how none of the past mattered but only the future with them to love her, protect her, and be by her side. Maybe when they explained about the money she now had it would make her feel better and more independent?

"Max?" He heard his name and looked up from the desk in his office. Alicia was visiting him at work. He stood up immediately and got to her so fast she stepped back.

"Are you okay? Is anything wrong?" he asked, sliding his hands up and down her arms, ensuring she was in one piece.

She chuckled.

"Of course I am. Isn't it safe here in your department?" she teased him.

He gave her a sideways glance and she smiled.

His brothers came in next.

"Hey, are you free for lunch?" Monroe asked, placing his hands on Alicia's shoulders behind her.

"I can squeeze in lunch," he said and walked back to his desk. He closed up the file and grabbed his keys.

He smiled as he wrapped his arm around her waist and escorted her out of the office with his deputies and staff members giving well wishes and telling them to enjoy lunch. They had been so supportive to Alicia when she was in the hospital and weeks later as she recovered. If he ate any more pie he would need to eat only vegetables for a week.

He smiled as they headed outside.

"Where should we go? The diner?" Max asked.

"Fiona's?" Monroe suggested and Alicia shook her head.

"Home. To our place," she told them as she hugged Max's side.

His heart raced with anticipation. Alicia had still been adjusting to living with them, but hearing her refer to home as hers, too, made him happy.

"I think we can salvage something to eat," he teased.

"Are you kidding me? We still have dinners frozen and just this morning Margaret Stoll sent over a chicken casserole and homemade biscuits. I'm going to need to start increasing my miles jogging," she said and they chuckled.

"You're not the only one. I may be joining you," Caldwell told her and hugged her side. They got into the truck and Monroe and Caldwell followed.

Max kept glancing at her as they drove.

"I heard back from the attorneys today," he told her.

"I don't want to talk about it. You know I don't care about what Tony tried to scam. It was bad enough having my brother show up at the hospital and then try to put up a GoFundMe link on Facebook to raise money for me. Thank God Monroe found that and stopped the funding."

He reached over and touched her hand. He held it and brought it over his thigh.

"It's been rough, but with our lawyers on board we ensured that we could end all of this."

She looked at him.

"End it all? You think you did?"

He nodded his head as he pulled the truck into the driveway between the two entry pillars and over toward the detached garage.

Monroe opened her door and helped her out. They headed into the house and to the kitchen.

"So what did the lawyers say?" she asked. Monroe and Caldwell stopped what they were doing.

"You heard back from them?" Caldwell asked.

"Just before you guys showed up at the department." He looked at Alicia.

"It's over, Alicia. Tony will be in jail for quite some time for the crimes he committed against you and others. The DA from Dallas is involved, too. But none of that is your concern. The papers he wanted to force you to sign weren't legal anyway. He was scamming you and hoping to scam some lawyers. The money was never his. It's all yours. Two hundred thousand dollars."

Her mouth dropped and she grabbed the counter.

"Holy shit," Monroe said.

Caldwell placed his hand on her shoulder.

"It's true, and it's safe and secure in an escrow account waiting for you to do whatever you want with it."

"For real?" she asked, sounding and looking shocked. He chuckled.

"For real."

She turned around and hugged Caldwell then she hugged Monroe.

She looked at Max and she suddenly looked serious.

"You left me that night at the construction site and set out to clear everything up and help free me from all of this. You and Monroe and

Caldwell are my heroes, my strength, my determination, and my everything. You dared me to succeed, to achieve my dreams by helping me any way you could, and I will love you forever for doing all of it." She hugged him and he smiled wide, hugged her back, and looked at his brothers who had love and respect in their eyes. They'd found their soul mate, their lover, and the woman of their dreams.

She pulled back.

"So, what should we have for lunch?" he asked. Caldwell and Monroe started naming all the things that were in the refrigerator, but their woman seemed to have a different idea as she pulled her camisole up and over her head.

"How about me?" she said.

Max pointed his finger at her as Caldwell hugged her from behind and cupped her breasts. He was licking her neck and suckling against her skin.

"Someone feeling naughty?" he asked.

She held his gaze.

"Real naughty, Sheriff Gordon. I think you better bring your handcuffs."

She slipped from Caldwell's hold and ran for the stairs. They followed hooting and hollering about spanking her ass and filling her with cock.

Max hurried along, too, and when they got to the bedroom she was stripping off her clothes and raising her hands in the air as if under arrest.

He pulled off his clothes in record speed as did his brothers and grabbed the handcuffs.

"Oh, little missy, you are in serious trouble."

Max turned her around by her hips as Monroe climbed on the bed. Max ran his hands up her hips over her breasts then to her arms and wrists. He locked them together with one hand, letting his cock slowly tap against the crack of her ass. She moaned.

Caldwell dropped the tube of lube on the bed them climbed up, stroking his cock. "I got a little appetizer for you, sweetness, and that naughty little mouth."

Monroe lifted her by her hips and impaled her onto his cock. She moaned and lowered but Max clicked on the handcuffs and held them in the center.

"Hot damn, she's pouring cream all over me. She likes this."

Max bent back and slapped her ass. She moaned louder.

"Fuck, we should have done this sooner. Damn she looks so fucking sexy like this," Caldwell said then cupped her breast and pinched the nipple. She rocked her hips and Max pressed her back lower as he spread her ass.

"I like having this control over you. You're our prisoner," Monroe told her as he held her hands above his head, causing her breasts to push together as he suckled them. Caldwell moved into position to the side and coaxed her head to the right so she could suck his cock.

"I've got to feel you, baby. I need that mouth."

She licked along Caldwell's cock and began to suck him deeper. As Max watched the three of them get into their own rhythm and absorbed the sounds of moans and desire fill the room, he grabbed the lube, pressed some into her ass, and absorbed everything about the moment.

"You're ours, Alicia. Ours forever."

He pulled fingers from her ass and replaced them with his cock. As he slowly pushed in, his brothers joined the new rhythm as Alicia moaned and rocked her hips. Monroe was kissing her wrists where the handcuffs remained and the sight sent Caldwell over the edge. He pumped his hips and came in her mouth. Max ran his hands along her shoulders and traced the gunshot wound with his finger. She looked over her shoulder.

"I need you, Max. Always," she said.

154 Dixie Lynn Dwyer

"And we need you," Monroe replied and both of them began a series of long, deep strokes that had Alicia screaming out her release and them following soon after.

As they cleaned her up and he removed the handcuffs, kissing her wrists and then her mouth, she smiled.

"I can get used to this," she said to them. Monroe trailed a fingernail along her breasts as Caldwell ran his palm along her belly and mound.

"Used to sex for lunch?" Caldwell teased. Monroe and Max chuckled.

"Used to being restrained with my handcuffs?" Max teased then stroked her pussy.

She wiggled and slapped at his hand. He pointed his finger at her, reprimanding her, and she stuck her tongue out at him. Monroe and Caldwell chuckled.

"Later, you'll get a spanking for that."

"Promises, promises," she replied.

"Oh you will," he said.

"As I was saying, I could get used to this. To making love to my men in the afternoon, or any time I want to."

They smiled.

"We might not get any work done."

"We'll figure it out. Life is perfect now. I have the three of you."

Max's heart lifted with joy. He and his brothers found the woman of their dreams and she was safe and secure with them always.

Epilogue

The smell of a hazelnut latte and some sweet buns filled her senses as Alicia worked on her latest masterpiece. The people coming and going, quietly watching her technique and waiting on the end results, didn't bother her anymore. Her heart was no longer heavy, her stresses good ones as she tried to complete orders, and also prepared for her first gallery showcase right in Charlotte.

Her dreams were becoming a reality. She was an independent entrepreneur. She used part of the money from her original store sale to pay off the mortgage Caldwell and Monroe held for her despite their resistance. That had cost her a few spankings, some creative techniques in bed, and finally some promises of fulfilling their deep dark sexual fantasies to get them to allow such a business move on her part, but it was all worth it, and actually she found out she really liked spicing up the sex in the bedroom. Especially the sex toys, the role-playing, and being restrained and spanked. Her men seemed to really like it, too.

She smiled wide as she finished the last piece to the stained glass she was working on. It was a custom order for a couple in New York who had a winery and wanted a similar piece to the one she made for her men months ago. As she thought about how this relationship started and how often they used the wine-tasting table to taste her instead, she couldn't help but feel like life was a gift and she was living a dream. Her men taught her so much. They taught her about never giving up, about what being cared for and loved was really all about, and they dared her, encouraged her, and helped her in every way to succeed and to find that fight within her that was always there but needed to be coaxed out of her.

She chuckled.

They sure did know how to coax a lot of things out of her.

She glanced to the right and there were Monroe and Caldwell. Looking sexy and smiling as they drank some coffee and talked with the customers. Max was standing outside by the patrol truck keeping an eye on things and making sure she was protected and safe. She'd found everything she ever wished for and needed in this town called Chance. It all happened because she made that first step of change by leaving Dallas and going after her dream. Life just didn't get any better than this. She was happy and in love and everything else was icing on the cake.

THE END

WWW.DIXIELYNNDWYER.COM

ABOUT THE AUTHOR

People seem to be more interested in my name than where I get my ideas for my stories from. So I might as well share the story behind my name with all my readers.

My momma was born and raised in New Orleans. At the age of twenty, she met and fell in love with an Irishman named Patrick Riley Dwyer. Needless to say, the family was a bit taken aback by this as they hoped she would marry a family friend. It was a modern day arranged marriage kind of thing and my momma downright refused.

Being that my momma's families were descendents of the original English speaking Southerners, they wanted the family blood line to stay pure. They were wealthy and my father's family was poor.

Despite attempts by my grandpapa to make Patrick leave and destroy the love between them, my parents married. They recently celebrated their sixtieth wedding anniversary.

I am one of six children born to Patrick and Lynn Dwyer. I am a combination of both Irish and a true Southern belle. With a name like Dixie Lynn Dwyer it's no wonder why people are curious about my name.

Just as my parents had a love story of their own, I grew up intrigued by the lifestyles of others. My imagination as well as my need to stray from the straight and narrow made me into the woman I am today.

For all titles by Dixie Lynn Dwyer, please visit
www.bookstrand.com/dixie-lynn-dwyer

Siren Publishing, Inc.
www.SirenPublishing.com

Lightning Source UK Ltd.
Milton Keynes UK
UKOW06f1835261115

263616UK00015B/414/P